THE SIBERIAN ODYSSEY
OF HANS SCHROEDER

Also by
Ashis Gupta

NOVELS
Krishna, A Love Story
Rahul, A Different Love Story
Dying Traditions

SATIRE
The Acts of the Compassionates

POETRY
The Gospel according to Clarence Thomas
'For New Orleans' and Other Poems (Editor)

NON-FICTION
Ecological Nightmares and the Management Dilemma:
the Case of Bhopal
Indian Entrepreneurial Culture

THE SIBERIAN ODYSSEY
OF HANS SCHROEDER

ASHIS GUPTA

BAYEUX ARTS
DIGITAL-TRADITIONAL PUBLISHING

Publication: October 2014

Published in Canada by
Bayeux Arts Digital-Traditional Publishing
119 Stratton Crescent, SW
Calgary, Canada T3H 1T7

www.bayeux.com

Cover and Book Design by Lumina Datamatics, Inc.

Library and Archives Canada Cataloguing in Publication

Gupta, Ashis, 1940-, author
The Siberian odyssey of Hans Schroeder / Ashis Gupta.

ISBN 978-1-897411-82-7 (pbk.)

I. Title.

PS8613.U68S52 2014   C813'.6   C2014-902244-1

The ongoing publishing activities of Bayeux Digital-Traditional Publishing under its varied
imprints are supported by the Canada Council for the Arts, the Government of Alberta,
Alberta Multimedia Development Fund, and the Government of Canada through the Book
Publishing Industry Development Program.

Printed in Canada by Friesens

To Shona and Arjun

1

Through the window over my bed, the world made no sense at all. Night was the only time I ever got to see through it, a stained piece of glass covered outside with strands of barbed wire. I remembered the view as dark and featureless, and I found it reassuring to see it unchanged each night. Sometimes when the frost lay heavy on the leafless shrubs outside my window and the pale moon ducked in and out of the clouds as I looked, a string of crystals exploded with points of fire if I moved my eyes. If I looked straight ahead, the blackness seemed to swallow it all, a blackness that turned the snow covering the earth to a dull, smoky grey, never white.

A strange thing happened one night. I looked outside and saw a faint glow punctuating the night in the distance. I was curious, but it remained a mystery to me for a long time. So much of my prison was a mystery. We set out to make the world our own and ended up grovelling for food, fighting off mice and stray dogs so as not to starve. To me, the barking of the dogs became the voice of God.

I've heard the voice of God from time to time. The last time I heard him the voice sounded somewhat faint, like a call from a faraway place. I thought about it for a long time, until the mice took over. Now they run in and out of the corners of my mind. Yes, mice have been very much on my mind the last few days. I hate mice. They're sly, small, crafty. You never win against mice.

Wiesbaden was free of mice when I was growing up. The very idea would've been intolerable. Nobody thought of mice in those carefree days of our youth.

At first we lived in a particularly elegant part of town. I never much cared for it. I fancied I was a wanderer. There wasn't a single corner of the town I didn't know. I don't recall ever seeing a mouse anywhere during my childhood. I suppose they must've been around. Mother used to tell me about grown men, and women of course, scavenging for food with stray cats and dogs before I was born. That was after the war I didn't know, when the British blockaded our ports. Maybe the cats chewed up all the mice by the time I was plucked out of my mother's womb in 1921.

I loved Wiesbaden. My earliest memories are those of its fabulous wide-open avenues, shining buildings from which I expected royalty to step out any moment, and rolling parks where the grass was always soft and green. At first, I could never understand why I saw so many big men in Wiesbaden. They were old men, fat men, hand in hand with old women, fat women. It was much later that I understood they were there to look and feel younger, to act younger as well. They said you came to Wiesbaden on crutches and left dancing the Charleston. As a child, that didn't seem a good enough reason for me to drink the terrible waters of the Kochbrunnen and the Adlerquelle. I refused to be tempted even by the music. During summer, the pavilion built over the Kochbrunen rang with music from the band.

The band started precisely at eleven each morning while the tourists sipped their 'chicken broth' in search of their lost youth. But not me.

I think Mother worked too hard for me. I remember her working at the Restaurant Neroberg not far from where we lived in a small apartment on the Roderstrasse. We could never have lived in that beautiful house if Father wasn't employed there as something of a jack-of-all-trades, a combination caretaker, gardener, and janitor. I would wait for Mother every evening in the restaurant lobby, for her to finish her chores and walk home with me. I was always careful to be well dressed at that time, so as not to embarrass Mother or be scolded by the waitresses coming in for the evening.

Sometimes she was late. Impatient, I would walk away and wander over to the Greek Chapel. I knew the chapel and the grounds by heart. I walked slowly on the marble floor, waiting to hear the soft echoes of my footsteps, until I stood facing the statue of the Duchess. Then I would turn back and head for the restaurant, careful not to be caught casting curious glances at the trees and the surrounding woods where lovers embraced at dusk and stayed until the evening star rose above the gilded domes of the chapel. Usually, Mother would be waiting in the lobby when I came back. She knew where I had been, and didn't seem to mind.

By the time Mother moved on to a job at the Hotel Vier Jahreszeiten, I was going to a school near the police station on Friedrichstrasse. There was a small playground which opened onto the road leading to Biebrich. During the day, my heart lay in Biebrich. That's probably why I remember so little of what they taught me at school. One of Father's friends once caught me lying on the beach opposite to Biebrich on a small island in the centre of the river. I should've been in school at the time. My back was sore for days after the thrashing Father gave me that night. I longed to lie on the warm sand with the beautiful men and women who lay there all summer, but I never made it. Still, I spent many hours there looking at them and admiring the Rhine boats that glided in and out of the wharf at Biebrich. My heart swelled thinking of what they might see as they travelled up and down the Rhine. Maybe they could catch sight of the Rhinemaidens who were real people as far as I was concerned. I still think they're real.

Father spoke very rarely to me. In fact, I don't remember him saying much even to my mother. He lost his caretaker's job one day and he was angrier than I had ever seen him. Some of the boys at school spread the word that he had been drinking too much and the gardens surrounding the apartment were beginning to look unkempt. We passed through some very unhappy days until Father finally found a job at the hospital. He quarrelled a lot during that time. At first I felt sorry for Mother because she cried when she was alone and walked to her job in the restaurant with bloodshot eyes. I think that was when I stopped going to meet her after work in the evenings. I no longer felt sorry for her. I've never felt sorry for her since. That's not quite true. Lately, I've begun to feel sorry for her all over again.

Wiesbaden was a happy, festive town. There was something brittle about it though, especially about the hordes of Englishmen and Americans so desperate about their fading youth. They told me that travellers had been coming for the baths and the Kur ever since the Romans established a settlement there and called it Mattiacum. I remember seeing traces of their architecture but can't remember seeing any Romans. Not real Romans, that is, clad in breastplates and armour, sword held high. But their spirits lay everywhere, and sightings were common. I often lit a cigarette in the shadow of the Heidenmauer, the ancient covered archway in the centre of town, and wondered how many Romans discovered eternal youth in Wiesbaden. I hoped they found relief from gout and sciatica at least. It's funny, every other person in America seems to be suffering from these ills.

The Hotel Vier Jahreszeiten where Mother worked was a splendid place, full of ghosts once again. In happier days she told us of the spirits of Prussian generals striding restlessly up and down its endless corridors, of the sound of laughter and the swelling notes of crystal touching crystal when the large halls were all dark and everything else was quiet. What I liked most about Mother's hotel was the dance hall. I first went there when I was fifteen, not to dance, but to admire its rich curtains, the marble floors, and the gilded arches. That must've been where I first learnt the meaning of passion - Siegfried's, Brunnhilde's. I quickly realised I could be anyone I wished inside the walls of the opera house. I could fall in love with anyone I wished.

The only other place in Wiesbaden that took my breath away was the Opera House. The first time I went there I saw *Tannhauser*. From that moment on, I became a slave to Wagner's music. Only Wagner could hold my heart in a grip of steel and hurl it to the top of the highest mountain, the depth of the deepest passions. The next time I was there, they did *Siegfried*. Before long, I was Siegmund and Siegfried. Much later, I even began to feel one with Wotan. In between, and afterwards, I spent countless hours sitting on the back entrance steps facing the garden called Warmer Damm, listening to muffled strains of music, dreaming of Brunnhilde's face etched in the evening sky. There was a statue of Schiller in front of the spot where I used to sit. It always intrigued me, but I never got around to finding out much about Schiller. I envied him though. Envied him the splendid gardens where he stood, envied him the strains of music that wove magic in the air and often transformed the spot into Valhalla itself.

It all seems like a dream now as I sit here in the midst of strangers. Some I know, others I don't care for. The sun begins to bother me as I sit down. As I move my chair closer to that of attorney Piscitelli's, he tells me to sit up. I guess I had gone back to sitting with my shoulders hunched. Doesn't create a good impression, he says. I watch the jurors enter the courtroom one by one and take their seats. They watch me. My face is in the shadows once more. It feels cool and my thoughts can return to mice. Yes, I don't remember seeing any mice in Wiesbaden. But back to God, I expect I'll hear from him soon.

2

It's hard to say if Hans heard from God or not. As he told me his story, there shone a strange light in his eyes. I was afraid to question what he obviously believed to be the truth. Sometimes, as I opened my mouth to add a comment or question a minor detail, I wished I could be the voice of God, resolute and overwhelming. At other times, I wished it were possible to enter Hans Schroeder's mind like a mouse and chew off bits and pieces of his secrets. But Hans himself doesn't seem to know much of his own secrets. He doesn't stash them away in secret hiding places. They're strewn all over his mind. Only God can pick his way through the trash and discover anything worthwhile.

I watched him out of curiosity, baffled by him, a warm, steamy day in September. His face sullen, his eyes unfocused, Hans Schroeder sat in the midst of strangers. He was not a tall man. Of medium height, there was a rugged strength about him that made strangers look at him just one more time. Some of the strangers in the courthouse were his acquaintances, not close, but acquaintances just the same. Now he seemed to look through them all. During one of the breaks, he told me they didn't care for him, nor he for them.

The thick, glistening wall of green which surrounded the courthouse, and the cool breeze rustling through the leaves made the day seem deceptively pleasant. Sunlight streamed in through the high courtroom windows, lit up the old stains on the desks and benches, and spread in dark shadows over the floor. So easy to fall asleep on a day like this. That's exactly what Hans seemed to be in danger of giving in to. Sleep.

The court Clerk, Tom Murphy, looked around the courtroom with short, jerky movements of his head until his eyes met those of Judge Collins. Then he stopped. The Judge nodded and Murphy threw back his head and shoulders and called out, "Hans Schroeder, you are now sent to the Bar to be tried, and these good men and women whom I shall call on to pass between the Commonwealth and you open your trial. If you would object to any of them, you will do so as they are called and before they are sworn. You have the right to challenge sixteen of the jurors without giving any reason therefor, and so many of the others as you have good cause for challenge. You may be seated."

"Mr. Clerk," said Judge Collins, addressing Tom Murphy, "will you direct the Crier to make proclamation to the Traverse Jurors."

"Mr. Crier," said Tom Murphy, "make proclamation to the Traverse Jurors."

"Ye good men and women of our County of Plymouth who have been summoned here this day to serve as Traverse Jurors, give answer to your names at first call," said the Crier. Then Tom Murphy called out each name and the jurors answered back.

The call completed, Judge Collins sat back in his chair and looked around him. Lean, grey haired and distinguished, Judge Collins was a fine-looking person as ever walked through the halls of Harvard Law School. "Well, ladies and gentlemen," he said, "you have been summoned to this sitting of the Superior Court, County of Plymouth, to serve as jurors in the trial of the two indictments of the Commonwealth against Hans Schroeder, as defendant, who is charged in indictment returned by the Grand Jury with the murder of Eva Schroeder, and in a second indictment with the murder of Katarina Schroeder, on or about the second day of November, in the year of our Lord nineteen hundred sixty six at Kingston, in the County of Plymouth.

"The case will be prosecuted by the Assistant District Attorney, Brian Concannon. The attorney, counsel for the defendant, is Mr. Patrick Piscitelli. I intend to speak to you this morning concerning the nature of your jury services and the duties of the court and the jury respectively in the trial of these homicide cases.

"No useful purpose will be served by attempting to anticipate questions in the trial of the cases that will come before us, but there are certain fundamental principles relating to the selection and duties of jurors which may be appropriately mentioned at this time.

"Jury service is an important public service. So important is it that the citizens of our Commonwealth for more than one hundred eighty years have willingly accepted it as compulsory public service. Jury service involves some degree of sacrifice. But sacrifice in the cause of jury service has been made many, many times, many thousands of times, by jurors who have preceded you here and will be made by many others who will follow. Here and now you are the trustees of that tradition. In the Massachusetts Constitution, our forefathers declared that this method of procedure - to have trial by jury afforded to all individuals living within the borders of the Commonwealth - is a sacred trust. You are custodians of that sacred trust. Its reputation is for you to guard. I am certain that you will guard and preserve our jury system as guardians of that sacred trust and transmit it to others who will come after you as jurors undiminished in its prestige and respect.

"It has salways been expected that the duties comprehended by jury service will be discharged by persons from all walks of life, taken from different communities within the County, endowed with varying abilities, unequal in experience, and probably accustomed to regard the same problems with different points of view. The function of a jury is to find the truth of events and happenings or transactions that occurred sometime in the past. In a broad sense, jurors are historians, but restricted in their search on the evidence presented to them in the courtroom by witnesses, and what they observed on a view if a view is taken in a case. None will be taken in this case.

"It is for the jury, not for the Court or the Judge to decide whether witnesses are to be believed. The jury has the exclusive right and the whole responsibility of deciding the facts. The law imposes upon the jury the responsibility of ascertaining the facts in dispute. The jurors are the sole judges of the facts, and the court or the judge may not interfere with their unfettered exercise of that prerogative.

"But the judge presiding at a trial has his own distinct functions. He is no mere referee or umpire between the parties. In discharging the functions of his office, the judge is required by the law to be the directing and controlling mind during the course of the trial. He is not a mere functionary to preserve order or to lend ceremonial dignity to the proceedings.

"Among those things that a judge has to do is to determine whether the evidence is to be submitted to the jury or excluded from their consideration, whether the evidence submitted by the respective parties is admissible or not admissible, in accordance with rules of law which have become more or less well settled and familiar to the legal profession. Of course, sometimes a rule may be clear but its applicability may raise a question. And the judge must instruct the jury at the conclusion of the evidence and after the arguments of counsel upon the principles of law which the jury are to consider in reaching their verdicts.

"Among the most important duties of the judge is, so far as possible, to see that a fair-minded, unbiased and unprejudiced jury is provided for the trial of criminal cases. Impartial justice to the best of the ability and understanding of the judge and the jury is the desired end in every case. The administration of justice by an impartial judge and an impartial jury has been basic to our conceptions of freedom and justice for many generations. It is the concern not merely of the immediate parties in the particular case or cases before the court, but its assurance is everyone's concern. The safety of society from lawlessness and crime, the security of the innocent from unjust accusations depend alike upon wise and impartial justice. As the Old Testment prudently admonishes us, to show partiality in judgement is not good.

"In the performance of his duties, therefore, a juror must cast aside all considerations of race, colour, religion, nationality, position in the community, and all other circumstances which may pertain as mere accidentals to the persons in the case. Nor should he be affected or influenced by prejudice or sympathy for the various parties or witnesses or the relatives of the deceased or of alleged victims, or of counsel. Meritorious jury service demands the absolute disregard of all considerations except of doing justice according to law. This honourable purpose each juror should resolve to cherish.

"Now, in order to provide for the trial of the murder indictments in the cases we are about to try, each of you, in accordance with custom, will be called singly, individually into the courtroom to be examined under oath to learn, as the statute provides, for whether you are related to the defendant or to the alleged victims, the deceased, or have an interest in the case, or have formed an opinion, or are sensible of any bias or prejudice. The examination will also determine whether the juror holds any opinion such as to preclude him from finding a defendant guilty of a crime punishable by death. The purpose of the examination of each person as he or she is called is to ascertain simply whether he or she stands impartial between the Commonwealth and the defendant on the issues to be tried on the indictments.

"If you are chosen as a juror, you will take an oath that you will well and truly try and true deliverance make between the Commonwealth and the prisoner at the bar according to the evidence. In the trial, you will hear the evidence of the Commonwealth and the evidence of the defendant, then arguments of counsel on both sides of the case. And at the conclusion of the arguments, the court, that is to say the presiding judge, will instruct you with respect to the law. You will be required to determine the facts in your deliberations in the jury room and to apply the law as it was given to you by the court. And then your duty will be to return a verdict, a true and just verdict according to the facts as you found them to be and the law as given to you by the court.

"You the jurors who are chosen will give your most painstaking and conscientious consideration to all the evidence. Justice and the desire to find the truth demands that. And it will be the jury's sacred duty to stand between the Commonwealth and the defendant with unbending impartiality and unflinching courage, guarding the rights of each with the utmost care and caution in order that truth may be established and thereby justice attained. Weakness and shirking one's duty as a citizen are disgraceful qualities of which I am confident you will not be guilty. Only by doing your duty according to law can your conscience be satisfied.

"In accordance with ancient practice, justified as well by modern conditions, during the selection of the panel you will be examined singly by the judge in this courtroom. That is to say, one at a time. The rest of you will be outside in the other room. I cannot imagine anything more cowardly than for a citizen who is a prospective juror to desire to avoid a public duty, that is to say, jury duty, by falsely asserting a bias or prejudice or the existence of opinions and views about the guilt or innocence of the defendant, or upon the subject of capital punishment, for the purpose of avoiding jury duty.

"On the other hand, nothing could be worse than for a prospective juror to conceal such views in order that he may serve on a jury with a biased and prejudiced mind. I assure you that the court is not offering or suggesting a way out of serving on this jury panel. It is desirable, however, to make clear to you what should be in your minds when you answer certain questions which the court will put to you, each of you whose names are drawn from the jury box by the Clerk.

"I want you to understand the questions now, because it will save time later. You will observe that some of these questions can be answered categorically. That is, they can be answered yes or no. Here are the questions that I shall put to you as they relate to this case. This will not preclude my asking additional questions if it occurs to me or if suggested to me and I accept the suggestions from counsel. The questions are: Are you related to the defendant, Hans Schroeder, the deceased, Eva Schroeder, or the deceased, Katarina Schroeder?

"The next question. Have you any personal interest in the case? And the next will be: Have you formed or expressed any opinion as to the guilt or innocence of the accused? The fourth question. Are you conscious of any bias or prejudice in relation to this case? The fifth.

Have you any opinion that would prevent you from finding a defendant guilty of an offense punishable by death? The sixth. Do you have any views on capital punishment that would prevent you from finding a defendant guilty of an offense punishable by death even though you were convinced on the evidence of his guilt beyond a reasonable doubt?

"There is one other question I intend to put to you. That question is: If the evidence permits a finding that the defendant is guilty of murder, and the evidence further warrants a finding that the defendant had a mental disease at the time of the alleged crime, and that as a result of this mental disease he did not have substantial capacity to conform his conduct to the requirements of law, have you any opinions that would prevent you from finding the defendant not guilty by reason of insanity? That, in substance, is the other question I intend to put to you.

"Elaborating on these questions, let me say that the first is a very simple question, whether you are related to the defendant or to either of the alleged victims, the deceased. And the second question asks if you have any personal interest in the case. Notice I emphasize the word 'personal'. Your answer might logically and honestly be yes, because I assume that if any of you have heard of the case or even if you have not heard of it, you might have a natural interest in it. But you will understand that by the word 'interest' in this question we mean a personal interest. That is to say, an interest of a personal nature, and not just normal curiosity.

"The next question is whether you have formed or expressed any opinion as to the guilt or innocence of the defendant. Common sense dictates that it is impossible to avoid forming some sort of an impression about a case. I don't mean this case but any case, concerning which newspapers have reported in its preliminary stages. And it would be impossible, I suppose, in many cases to find a citizen who has not read about a case or has thought about it even for a short time. By the word 'opinion', ladies and gentlemen, in this question we mean not an original impression. What is meant is a conclusion based on thought or, as the Supreme Judicial Court has put it, a candid judgement. Such an opinion would be one that you honestly could not change or alter. If, however, the opinion or original impression formed or expressed by you is of such a nature that it would not consciously preclude you from following the evidence and returning a verdict based on the evidence, based on the testimony given under oath, and the exhibits admitted in evidence, then you are not disqualified.

"The next question is whether you are conscious of any bias or prejudice with relation to the case. Well, in this Commonwealth we know of no distinction of race, creed or colour in the administration of justice. And whatever you may have heard about other jurisdictions, we in the Commonwealth of Massachusetts pride ourselves that in our courts all persons stand alike. If you are aware of any bias or prejudice or bigotry for or against the defendant which would preclude you from rendering a fair verdict based on the evidence and the law, you should declare it to the court. And by the same token, if you have prejudice against the prosecution or the prosecuting officers, you should so state to the court.

"By these, the last two questions, the law intends to exclude any person who has made up his mind or formed a judgement in advance for either side, the Commonwealth or the defendant. But the opinion or judgement must be something more than a vague impression formed from casual conversation with others or from reading imperfect or abbreviated newspaper accounts. It must be such an opinion upon the merits of the case as would be likely to be biased or prevent a candid judgement after a full hearing of the evidence.

"Now, the next question you will be asked is whether or not you hold any views that would prevent or preclude you from rendering a verdict of guilty of an offense punishable by death. Or, putting it another way, do you have any views of capital punishment that would prevent you from finding a defendant guilty of an offense punishable by death even though you were convinced on the evidence of his guilt beyond a reasonable doubt. You will bear in mind, ladies and gentlemen, that it is still the law of this Commonwealth that murder in the first degree is punishable by death. If you have any opinion against capital punishment, then you must ask yourself whether that opinion would conscientiously prevent you from finding the defendant guilty even if you could be convinced of his guilt, beyond a reasonable doubt, of the crime of murder in the first degree. It may be that some of you would prefer that the laws of the Commonwealth should be changed to abolish capital punishment. But by itself, that opinion should not preclude you from serving as jurors in this case. Other jurors have entertained such a belief, yet have courageously and fairly discharged their duties in accordance with the law, uninfluenced by their private beliefs. It is only when a juror could not under any circumstances, notwithstanding the evidence and its strength, find a defendant guilty of an offense punishable by death that he would be ineligible to serve.

"Finally, if the evidence permits a finding that the defendant is guilty of murder, and the evidence further warrants a finding that the defendant had a mental disease at the time of the alleged crime, and as a result of that mental disease he did not have substantial capacity to conform his conduct to the requirement of law, have you any opinions that would prevent you from finding the defendant not guilty by reason of insanity?

"When I refer in these questions to opinions it is not every opinion or impression formed by a person in advance of trial that renders a juror ineligible. The examination of jurors is intended to exclude only those persons who have prejudged the case and have formed a firm judgement in advance, for one side or the other. In a metropolitan area today, the ordinary person cannot altogether escape the impact of the media. The media can't possibly give full accounts of happenings that result in court trials. So, mere opinions formed from the media or from rumors, or from speculation concerning the alleged contention of the prosecution and the defense, or as those contentions have been officially stated during preliminary hearings and proceedings in court, such opinions are not enough to excuse jurors.

"Perhaps it isn't necessary to remind you that the questions asked of you must be answered under oath. They must be answered not as you might wish to answer to escape a weighty responsibility of public service, but as they must be answered to disclose the truth under inquiry.

"You should keep in mind that you are selected in the same manner and from the same source that countless jurors who have served with distinction in the past were selected and drawn. There is no reason to suppose that matters of great importance have been or will be submitted to persons more intelligent, more competent, or more impartial than you. And if you remain conscious of your responsibilities of public service that now rest upon you, I am confident you will respond to the call of duty courageously and with high-minded purpose."

The judge looked around the sunny courtroom. At the defendant, lost in thought, scowling at no one in particular. At the prospective jurors, stone-faced men and women. At the curious and excited visitors. At counsel, Pat Piscitelli, in a light grey suit, flanked by his brilliant assistant, Rob Klein, and Brian Concannon, confident in a blue, pin-stripe suit. "We will now take a short recess before the jury is empanelled," he said.

There was a flurry of noise and activity. A few minutes later it was as if no one had ever crossed the threshold of the courtroom in ages.

3

Is this a preamble to my fate? The grand trappings seem to be there, but none of the substance I am, was, used to. Still, I liked Judge Collins. His niceties were those I had grown up with. So charming and old-worldly. I guess I drifted further and further away from them as I left my childhood behind. I doubt that I was responsible for it. At first, even war was so charming.

Judge Collins reminded me of my father. Only in terms of his height and features, certainly not his wisdom. The judge is smart. My father, sadly, was a person of no consequence.

Everything's so tedious in this courtroom. So drab and tedious. Wish I could see my face in the mirror. I never drank that spurious spring water except once, but could it be I am still the handsome, strapping officer of the Grossdeutschland, the SS panzer division? Ah! we are such fools.

They were heady days, champagne galore from the caves of Henkell and Company. We walked around in heaven. Heaven was the Russian front. As I raised myself from the turret of my brand new Panther tank, I saw once again the outlines of distant Russian villages I had grown so accustomed to watching through the desolate winter and the awakening spring. All through winter, when the earth lay shrouded in white, I kept dreaming of the mighty river Don. But it was still a hundred miles or so away, and our forces had yet to eliminate the salient at Kursk.

I forgot the Don as the snow melted away and colour returned to the earth. Almost magically, I discovered forgotton valleys and streams that wound lazily through the land. Our camp, our little piece of land, was at the edge of the forest. One day I decided to walk into it all alone. Soon I was surrounded by trees on all sides. Then I found myself surrounded by whispered sounds. I must have fallen asleep. Suddenly, I started from my sleep at the sound of what could only have been a blast from Siegfried's trumpet. I started to walk over the damp dead leaves left exposed by the melting snow. I had no idea which way I was walking, but a curious sense of exhilaration deepened within me with every step. The more I walked the more certain I was I would stumble across some glorious apparition. The feeling stayed with me even after I had returned to camp several hours later.

And the nights grew tempting and mysterious. As I lay awake at night there were times I thought I could almost touch the stars. I did touch them, did I not, as I sat on the steps of the pavilion on the Neroberg, when Mother was late coming out of the restaurant, and pretended I was looking at the rising moon and not the lovers in the shadows? And when the infantry fell silent, I could even hear the gathering murmur of creeks replenished by the melting snow.

Our panzer division had been entrenched on the outskirts of Rylsk. The terrain directly in front of us was a gently rolling plain. As the weeks rolled by and the sun gathered strength, the land burst forth with new life besides the Russians we could easily see through our binoculars. The most spectacular life grew in the cornfields. The nights grew shorter, the sun grew stronger and the light shimmered more and more rapturously over the growing corn.

Death came to us that summer when we were least expecting it. It didn't take me long to get used to watching men die in battle. But it was something else watching the sick and the wounded die in the boxcars. The smell, I can still smell it off my body. That reeking hell of excrement where the dead often stood jammed with the living until the boxcar doors opened at some siding. Then we'd remove the dead to another car, a boxcar of the dead. While travelling from the disaster of the war front to the Russian camp at Etschige, I had often been ordered by the guards to help carry the dead. Stumbling through the banks of drifting snow seemed more endurable, doubled up under the weight of a body on my back seemed less painful than the sight of bodies piled one on top of the other in the boxcar of the dead.

What a harvest the Russians carried home that summer. When I moved under orders from one boxcar to another, I would occasionally look up in search of non-existent avenues of escape. Always it was the same sight, an endless line of boxcars dwindling darkly into the distance. The dogs and the double rows of flash-light carrying guards left no room for hope.

Back in the boxcar, the guards always flickered their lights around the walls in a final check. Then the heavy doors would slide shut, with at least two men on the inside lending their weight to lock the door of their own prison. With the lock in place, there always followed a dead silence as in the moment of closing a grave, with each prisoner straining his eyes through the darkness, looking uncomprehendingly at the door. Then the outside latch fell into place with the dead click of metal. As the scratching and clicking noises of the wire and chain further securing the door faded away, the fifty odd men in the small freight car tried to stir and stretch themselves as best they could.

All night the guards marched up and down the line of cars if we happened to be stopped at a siding. At regular intervals, a heavy tramping over our heads reminded us that patrols also marched the length of the train along the roof.

Our train moved along I believe from Kursk to Smolensk, a smouldering, ravaged city. It became colder as we moved north, and darker for longer and longer periods. The only entrance for light or air into our boxcar was a chute consisting of two sideboards jutting out from a hole cut low in one wall. This was our latrine. By the time the first rays of dawn sneaked through the chute, the iron strips on the walls and ceilings were coated with frost from our breathing.

Towards the end of our journey, we got stuck in an endless snowstorm. The snow blew through the chute all night long and gradually covered us all. We were so cold the snow did not melt even when it touched our bodies. We huddled against each other, not knowing when a neighbour had ceased to fight and slid quietly into death's arms. Life was a simple matter of surviving another day, another hour, within the four wooden walls of the boxcar, of not starving, not freezing, not dying from exhaustion.

Many times during that painful halt, we were called out for burial details. When it was my turn, I stumbled out to the Russians' hurry-up refrain, "Schnell, schnell, bnystro." There was no time to arrange the body for carrying. The wind ripped into our faces. From the boxcar to which we had been summoned, they rolled a woman's body into the blanket I and a fellow prisoner held between us. The head and arms bobbed and dangled from the blanket as we staggered to the end of the train. We lay the blanket on the ground as we came to a stop in front of the door of an immense boxcar. The door was stuck.

When the guards finally managed to open the door, we found the entire length of the boxcar covered with a pile of bodies, men and women, seven layers high and reaching almost halfway to the roof. The bodies beneath lay squeezed and almost flattened under the pressure from the top. The oozings of death lay frozen and congealed in the oddest places and in the strangest colours. The force needed to open the door had sheared the shoulder and arm from a corpse on the second layer, leaving the gaunt bone, still tight in its socket, dangling over the edge of the car.

I have seen death so often. I have seen the drippings of death form like molten wax on the faces of those I loved. And I've remained unmoved. I might be mistaken, but at times I was certain some of the guards were women. In my dreams and half-sleep I could almost believe that the women were carrying to some secret home the bodies of heroes slain in battle.

As I waited in front of the boxcar I thought I heard the wild music of the Valkyries whistling through the sky. Suddenly, I felt no pain.

Some prisoners were already on top of the pile of bodies. We heaved the corpse up to them and it landed at their feet. Then, like laborers filling a coal bin, they swung the body to the far end of the car where the pile had already reached the ceiling. They told me they had seen rats scampering through the bodies. Boxcars full of tons and tons of food for the dirty rascals while the rest of Europe starved. But I must confess I never saw those rats.

How quickly one got used to death. There were no heroes here. Simply rotting flesh.

4

ollowing the recess, attorney Piscitelli asked the
judge, "Your Honour, might you not ask the jurors
whether or not they have seen anything in the papers
concerning the case. A great deal of pre-trial publicity
has taken place in this instance. The defendant's picture has appeared in the *Brockton Enterprise* several
times."

Then, waving a newspaper in his hand, Piscitelli
continued, "Here's an article in the *Brockton
Enterprise*, dated July 17, 1972, showing a picture of
Mr. Schroeder. The article calls him a convicted axe
murderer, indicating he had earlier been sentenced
to the electric chair, that he was a former German
tank commander, and the like." Piscitelli picked up
another paper, "Here's one from July 19, 1972, again
referring to him as a convicted axe murderer in big,
bold, black type.

"And these other ones," said Piscitelli, pointing to
several other papers on the table by his side. "August
2, 1972, again axe murderer in big, bold, black type.
And this one is August 3, 1972, another one - convicted
axe killer to appeal bail denial. And more recently in
September, 1972, an article in the *Enterprise* stating
Mr. Schroeder was convicted on October 7, 1966, of
the murders of his wife and daughter and sentenced to
die in the electric chair, and that his sentence was then

commuted to life imprisonment and he won a new trial. That information is erroneous."

All this led Judge Collins to add another question to his list. Can you, in all good conscience, form a candid judgement or judgements on these indictments uninfluenced by such impressions as you may have formed from reading newspaper accounts, or hearing radio and television reports, or reports from any source whatsoever about this case?

Fred Sigren was the first prospective juror to be called. All went well with the judge's questioning of Sigren, a truck driver for the National Biscuit Company in Brockton, until he was asked, "Have you any physical disability which would impair your capacity to serve as a juror, bearing in mind that you might be absent from home if this becomes a protracted trial?"

"The only thing," began Fred Sigren haltingly, "is that my wife might go to the hospital anytime. She has been in the hospital three times this summer, and they told her she'd have to come back in six weeks, which six weeks is up now, to go through more tests. If they call her, then she'll be in hospital and I'll have to watch the little one. That's the only thing I can think of." Fred Sigren was excused.

Paul Dooley, a laborer in the State Department for Public Works in Brockton, was the next to be sworn in. He answered the judge's questions simply and clearly. The prosecution found him acceptable. But attorney Piscitelli noticed that the jury list showed him as being a manager. Questioned, Paul Dooley admitted that, until he went to work for the town as a laborer, he had indeed been a deli manager for the Brockton Public

Market. Piscitelli did not raise any objections to the juror.

Frank Gardner, a delivery clerk for the United Parcel Service from Plymouth was next called to the stand. He was challenged by the defense. So Francis Fiske was sworn in next. A delinquent bill collector for the Hancock Bank and Trust Company of Quincy. Judge Collins declared him prejudiced fairly early in the questioning. "Have you," asked the judge, "formed any opinion or opinions as to the guilt or innocence of the defendant so that your judgement would be affected in arriving at a true verdict based on the evidence you heard in court, and on that alone?" To which Frank Gardner replied, "Yes, I believe so."

Paul Griffin, a die setter for the Lite Control Corporation of Hanson was the next juror. And so they came, butcher, plumber, school teacher, and housewife. They were empanelled before long, all twelve of them, nine men and three women.

The indictment charged Hans Schroeder with murder in the first degree. But if the twelve weren't satisfied with the evidence, they could find Hans guilty of murder in the second degree. Judge Collins read to the jurors what murder was all about: "Murder committed with deliberately premeditated malice aforethought, or with extreme atrocity or cruelty or in the commission of a crime punishable by death or life imprisonment is murder in the first degree. Murder which doesn't appear to be murder in the first degree is murder in the second degree."

Judge Collins ruled that a principle of Constitutional Law applied to the case, as a result of which there could be no verdict of guilty of first degree murder based on a finding of murder deliberately premeditated. But the jury could still come up with a verdict of murder in the first degree if they found that Hans had killed with malice aforethought, and that the murder was committed with extreme atrocity and cruelty.

Members of the jury blanched as Judge Collins told them that the statute he had read defined degrees of murder but not murder. So he told them what he thought about murder. "Murder is the unlawful killing of a human being with malice aforethought. Murder is the malicious killing of a human being, and it has been truthfully said that one who intentionally, without palliation or excuse, takes the life of a human being does it maliciously. And that is the definition of second degree murder.

"In the case before you, if you find that the defendant committed murder then you have to consider whether the act was committed with extreme atrocity and cruelty. Then the verdict would be guilty of murder in the first degree. In the crime of murder, the killing of a human being must be unlawful. Not every killing, mind you, is unlawful. The simplest example is war.

"Malice aforethought is an interesting concept. Malice as used here doesn't necessarily imply hatred or ill will towards the person killed, but it has a more comprehensive meaning. It means not only hatred and revenge, but also every other unlawful or unjustifiable impelling force or intent which is in the mind of the killer which moves him to kill.

"If the wicked intention to do injury to another precedes the act by which the injury is done, it is malice aforethought. The wilful purpose of carrying out one's own evil desires and plans without regard for the rights of others is enough in itself to constitute malice aforethought.

"Malice is implied from any deliberate or cruel act, however slight. The practical test to apply in the murder case, to determine whether the killing was murder, is to ask yourself this question: Did the defendant unlawfully kill the deceased? If your answer is yes, then you have to ask: Was the killing done because of any wicked, corrupt or unjustifiable impelling forces or intent? If, again, your answer is yes, then the killing was murder. If your answer is no, then the killing was not murder."

5

How dull, I thought. Yet, how essential. How funny. So let me take you along for a walk, I said to my friend from the *Brockton Enterprise*. It is so easy to drift off to sleep. The proceedings really don't interest me that much. But there is this gnawing sadness inside me. I must have been mad. How could I have done what they say I did? I know what the verdict once was, what it will be this time. I'll accept it. I deserve it all. I don't know why I am fighting it. Pardon me if I slip away from it all from time to time. Come with me. Let me take you into the heart of time, into the living, nightmarish soul of my existence, I said.

You see, I didn't know who we were. I didn't know where we came from. We were in hell. Of this I had no doubt.

As we lowered ourselves out of the boxcars, a procession of haggard women came trudging up the track in our direction. They wore black bubushkas and dirty quilted dresses. Their feet were bound tightly in felt wrap-around boots. Slung over their shoulders were heavy iron picks and long wrenches. They looked at us without any curiosity and shuffled past without a word. I had to suppress a strong urge to laugh in their faces. The Valkyries never die, I thought. They simply grow old and get sent away to Russian prison camps.

We marched through ugly wooden palisades, about ten feet high, enclosing a square compound with watchtowers at each corner. The wide gate was mounted by a wooden arch carrying in crude Russian letters the inscription "Column Nine". The snow-covered rooftops I could see from outside the wall now revealed themselves as a collection of barracks ranged around a parade ground. Each barrack was a cabin about twenty four feet wide and perhaps eighty feet long. They were log cabins, with the chinks between the logs stuffed with peat plaster.

The rough wooden bunks inside were typical of the kotorgo, the Russian forced labour camps. The entire length of the cabin was heated by two primitive stoves placed near the ends. We were reminded at every opportunity that this was the Soviet Union - "Those who work, eat; those who don't, die."

Before long, many of us would die, but not for not working. The food, the cold, the wretched living conditions all conspired to wreak havoc with body and mind. For many of us, the colour of the body changed gradually from an angry red to sickly chocolate. These were victims of advanced cases of pellagra, where each hair root was a small reservoir of pus. Nothing helped, not even spoonfuls of black fish soup which we often saved to smear our bodies with and relieve the pain. Our minds changed too, but that was a different matter.

We all had to go through the medical hut. It was conveniently located near the women's barracks. Apart from the doctors and the technical people who seemed constantly to be going in and out of the hut, other members of the camp's hierarchy were never too far away.

The urkas, the bytoviks and the byelorutchki made up the social order. The urkas were mostly hardened criminals, the most frightening I could imagine. Every young girl coming into the camp passed through their hands before landing up in the beds of the camp chiefs.

There are things I remember, and things I fight in vain to recall. I was told that the first contingents of urkas to enter Russian camps quickly proclaimed within the camp zone, from dusk to dawn, a miniature prisoners' republic. They held their own trials and meted out justice in the night. They were especially harsh on political prisoners whose wisdom and intelligence were often fearsome and intimidating.

No guard would've dared to show himself inside the barracks after dark. They did nothing even when the piercing shrieks and moans of prisoners being slowly murdered could be heard all over the camp. Nobody, not even the guards, knew when an ugly billhook would appear behind one of the corners of the barracks and split his head open.

I seem to have lost count of how many years I actually spent in Russia. But, gradually, I was beginning to despair. Years in Siberia had taught me this meant death. It was easy to see death creeping in upon those who had given themselves up to despair and the thought of death. They seemed incapable of any resistance. Sooner or later, they ended up in the mortuary with personal data written on a slip of paper tied round the ankle.

Russians, Poles, Germans, the poison of despair left no one untouched. There was something uniform about the deaths of specific nationalities. Watching the Poles die was by far the most excruciating experience. Us Germans usually lapsed into endless, feverish deliriums. The Poles died suddenly, like birds falling off a branch in hard frost, or like some ocean fish which burst from inner pressure upon being brought to the surface from the deep. One short cough, one hardly audible gasp, followed by a tiny white cloud of breath which hung for a moment in the air. Then the head fell heavily on the breast, while the hands scraped the snow on the ground with one last movement.

I began to grow less and less afraid of death. I never wished it upon myself though. It was the anonymity of death which bothered me most. It was clear that, for most of us, death would be as insignificant as the passing of a fly in the middle of the night. We were troubled by the certainty that, when we died, no one would ever learn of our death, no one would know where we had been buried. The presence of death was so strong and convincing that every prisoner seemed to hide within the delicate shell of sleep from the menace stealing towards him across the neighbouring bunks, afraid to remind it of his still-pulsing existence by even the softest sigh. At other times, we made pacts with fellow prisoners about the survivor informing the others' families of the date of death and the approximate place of burial. There seemed to be a strange comfort in that, almost a final cry of defiance. The barrack walls were covered with the names of prisoners scratched in the plaster. Their friends were required to complete the date after their death by adding a cross and a date. With no one waiting for me outside, this ritual had no meaning for me.

In the first few months following my capture, I attempted to write home whenever the opportunity arose. While my fellow prisoners continued to write, often out of a sense of dread or desperation, I gave up writing altogether after the first year. There seemed nobody to write to. None of my letters ever brought back a reply. I could see that my fellow prisoners' letters to their loved ones were no more than a feeble assertion of life. If the regular pattern of letters stopped one day, it would probably have signalled a single message - death. I could think of no one who might be interested in such a message from me. My mother perhaps, but I had no idea whether she was dead or alive. After the first year or so, she simply ceased to exist for me.

I remember my last winter in Russia. The blizzards came sooner than usual that year. Now that there was little work to do once more, I spent a lot of time staring out of the window near my bunk. I suppose there were days when I could look outside from my bunk. I forget. I forget if it was day or night. When the snow blew, the snowflakes entangled themselves in the beams of the searchlight. Sometimes I thought the specks were the restless spirits of prisoners rising from the earth and reaching for the gods who sat above the clouds. The wind moaned and the trees creaked. And my thoughts drifted to Tulla. Tulla was beautiful. She had the perfect face. She had the flattest stomach I have ever seen. One night, I remember Klevshin and his cronies eating off her stomach - rough slices of bread under her breasts, a scoop of butter or whatever dumped on her navel. Tulla's home was a grave near the camp perimeter. Something grossly cruel about that. Why Tulla? There were dark rumours that Klevshin's body had also been thrown into the same grave. I would've gladly traded places with Klevshin.

On the second day in May, I forget the year, one of the officials came in with a great flurry and bellowed, "Hitler's dead! It's all in the papers. The Red Army has taken Berlin." I wasn't sure what to make of it at the time, or what it meant for me. I don't think I was too interested. I did feel a wrenching sensation around my heart. I think I felt the emptiness Wotan must've felt waiting for the death of Siegfried and the final end of Valhalla. Yes, my heart was heavy.

As winter deepened, the blizzards grew worse. At such times, long ropes were strung between the barracks and the mess hall so people wouldn't lose their way in a snowstorm. One evening, as I was battling the winds and working my way along the ropes towards supper, a fellow prisoner walking back along the same rope, stumbled into me. "Lucky you," he murmured. "Looks like you're going back to Germany, Hans."

With my eyes half shut against the wind, I couldn't be sure whether the Russian was mocking me or not. The thought of Germany sent shivers through my body. I quickly cautioned myself not to let my emotions get the better of me. I wanted to ask the Russian a question or two. But by the time I caught my breath and could turn my head and body around, the man was gone. It was only about another forty yards or so to the mess hall. That night, it seemed an eternity.

If I thought of the future, it was always in terms of other people. If and when I gave in to this preoccupation, it was with an odd, burning intensity for I was determined not to look at the future for myself. That was the way it was with my thoughts about returning to Germany.

Different Germans reacted differently to the prospect of returning home. Some were openly jubilant, others were more subdued. There were even three or four older men, sick and weary, who were far from certain of being alive on the day of their deliverance. I was one of those who grew nervous and withdrawn to the point where some of the Russians openly asked us if we would prefer to stay on in Yercevo.

The day of leaving finally arrived. The sight of the boxcars waiting for us at the nearby railway yard sent a chill of fear through my body. What was a little reassuring was that these carriages looked far less forbidding than those that had brought us to Etschige and Yercevo.

Faces, some known, mostly unknown, kept rising in my mind. They kept getting blurred and confused as the train rushed past an occasional burnt-out warehouse, a relic of the war, or a solitary barn, freshly painted and marking Russia's resurgence. I kept staring outside the carriage and tried to focus on the individual faces rushing through my mind until I began to feel dizzy. My legs began to shake and a sharp, excruciating pain shot through my head. I sat down on the floor, trying to hide the trembling in my body. Gradually the pain grew less. I touched my head and remembered the Russian interrogator who had struck me with his rifle butt in Etschige. I might be free, but I could never rid myself of his cruel eyes. Nor could I set myself free of the pity in Tulla's eyes, forever following me like a shadow.

I had begun to despair of ever being able to revive my faith in God. It seemed unnecessary when there was no hope. God was hope. When hope died, God died too. But many of my fellow prisoners walked with God. Often, I was surprised to see their flagging spirits revive miraculously. It's hard to know when I lost my God. There were times I thought I was close to rediscovering him. But I was fooling myself. What I needed was to rediscover myself, to crawl my way back through time. And that I could never do.

6

The assistant district attorney drew himself up to his full height and began his examination of Dr. Woodward. Mr. Concannon started with facts. "Doctor, I ask you to assume as true the following facts," he said. "That the defendant, Hans Schroeder, was born in Wiesbaden, Germany, on October 17, 1921, entered the German army at the age of seventeen in 1938, that he was captured by the Russians in 1944 and sent to a Russian prison camp. He remained there until 1947. Following his repatriation, he returned to Wiesbaden and worked as a bus driver among other things until August 1956. At that time he came to America with his family and became an American citizen in 1961. He had married Eva in 1949. There were four children. Katarina, born August 19, 1953, in Germany. Chris, born March 22, 1958. Dennis, born February 26, 1961. And Carolyn, born January 19, 1962.

"Following his arrival in America, he worked at various jobs, apparently steadily and conscientiously. From August 1961 to September 1966 he worked as a manager in an appliance center, earning about $125.00 a week. At that time, he obtained employment at the Lahey Gas Company in Wareham, earning about $150.00 per week. He continued at this job until the time of the alleged incident, which is the subject of the indictment in this case. There is no family history of mental illness, and no evidence of any prior psychiatric problems.

"Regarding his marriage, Schroeder stated to Dr. Graham, the admitting physician at Bridgewater, on November 7, 1966, that he had loved his wife up until three years ago. He wouldn't elaborate any further. He admitted he had had problems with her, that she was irritable, quarrelled frequently. Later, he said he was angry at her because of her inadequacy and her failure to become more American.

"Now consider this, Doctor. Mrs. Peggy Constanza has said that the defendant, Schroeder, told her he loved her as early as October 1965. She has said that in October 1966 he wrote her and said he loved her dearly. She said further that on two separate occasions in October and November 1969 Schroeder told her that he would kill himself and his family if she didn't go away with him.

"Bridgewater records show that Schroeder worked right up to the date of the offense. The admission note on November 7, 1966, states that he had been drinking heavily, and claimed to have become intoxicated, having fallen into a deep sleep and remembering nothing of the offense. Notes by various doctors state that, by his own admission, he had no recollection of any further event until being picked up by two hunters on November 6, 1966, in a semi-frozen condition and with vomit on his clothes. Dr. Wilkins on February 27, 1967, reported that Schroeder described no memory from the night before the crime until he woke up in the woods intoxicated, out of gas, and only two bottles of vodka in his car.

"Several witnesses at these hearings have testified to contact with Schroeder during the period from November 3, 1966, to November 6, 1966. Mrs. Constanza said that Schroeder telephoned her on the morning of November 4, 1966, saying that his wife and daughter were dead at home, that he was in Canada with the three children, and that he couldn't do it to the others. Stuart Jones testified that Schroeder phoned him to say that he had done something terrible, that his wife and daughter were dead at home. A police officer, Corporal Sanga, testified that he had been called, and when he saw Schroeder he asked if he was Hans Schroeder. Sanga testified that Schroeder responded, 'Yes, I am. I did it. I did it. I did it.'

"Mr. Pettit, on duty at the motel where Schroeder checked in with his children on November 3, 1966, testified that Schroeder signed in, paid the charges, that he was clean shaven, and that there was nothing unusual about him.

"On November 7, 1966, he was admitted to Bridgewater. He is then described as depressive, crying, with a headache, but responsive, coherent, cooperative, with no evidence of psychosis. It is stated that there was no overt, erratic, or psychotic behavior.

"On this same day, November 7, 1966, he gave extensive histories to two separate examiners, Dr. E. Graham, the admitting physician and Mr. Pierce, the social worker. He talked at length about everything but the tragedy. When the subject of the offense was brought up, he went into tears. The topic was therefore not pursued. According to Mr. Pierce, he was cooperative, oriented, exact as to dates and places, not paranoid, not psychotic, but in severe depression.

"Further hospital notes indicate that symptoms of depression continued when he was questioned about the offense. If this topic was avoided, he got along well. The more closely he was questioned, the more disturbed he would get. The diagnosis made at Bridgewater was psychotic depressive reaction.

"Based on these facts, Doctor, which I ask you to assume, do you have an opinion relative to the question whether or not Hans Schroeder was suffering from any mental illness prior to the alleged offense?"

Before Dr. Woodward could open his mouth, defense counsel raised his voice and said, "Just yes or no, please."

Dr. Woodward answered yes. That was the last word he was allowed to speak that day. Soon the court became embroiled in the admissibility or otherwise of the complete Bridgewater State Hospital records on Hans Schroeder. Pat Piscitelli contended that there were too many conflicting opinions in the hospital records. Besides, what the prosecution seemed to be doing was trying to elicit an opinion from Dr. Woodward with respect to opinions expressed by others.

"I make an objection to the whole admissibility of all of these," said defense counsel, "along with the many portions that should not go in because they deny a confrontation to the defendant and violate his constitutional rights. The person to whom these statements were supposedly made by the defendant is not available for confrontation by the defense counsel."

Before Dr. Woodward could return to the witness stand the following day, the entire matter of Hans Schroeder's prison medical records had to be resolved.

Finally, it succeeded in entering the court proceedings, subject to many objections and qualifications. Judge Collins said, "It may appear for the purposes of this hearing that the treatment of the defendant at Bridgewater State Hospital was for psychotic depressive reaction and an emotional, unstable personality. The hospital records are now admitted in evidence, subject to the objections and exceptions of the defendant based on constitutional objections pertaining to the confrontation of witnesses."

In the earlier trial, Schroeder had received two concurrent sentences of life imprisonment at the Massachusetts Correctional Institution in Walpole. His appeal to the Supreme Judicial Court of Massachusetts argued that various admissions and confessions he had made subsequent to the murders were involuntary and therefore inadmissible. Schroeder's appeal also argued that the statute defining murder with extreme atrocity or cruelty - that is, first degree murder, of which he was convicted - was vague, uncertain, and indefinite. The State Supreme Court held that Schroeder's statements had been properly admitted for the jury's consideration, and that the statute was not void for vagueness. Hans Schroeder's appeal failed.

In August, 1972, Schroeder filed a petition for writ of habeas corpus in the U.S. District Court for the District of Massachusetts. The petition repeated the arguments of the earlier appeal and alleged constitutional errors on the part of the trial court. The petition was denied without a hearing. Schroeder appealed this decision to a U.S. Court of Appeals. This time, the Court of Appeals reversed the trial court's admission into evidence of Schroeder's questionable statements, thereby also overturning the Judicial Court's ruling on the issue. A new trial was subsequently ordered.

Although the mandate of the U.S. Court of Appeals was issued in April, 1973, the Commonwealth of Massachusetts successfully blocked the setting of a new trial date. In fact, it would be September of that year before Schroeder's trial could begin. The attorney handling Schroeder's appeals at the time had been employed by the Massachusetts Defenders Committee. As such, he was subject to legal restrictions which barred him from defending Schroeder at the retrial on first-degree murder charges. The court therefore appointed Patrick Piscitelli as counsel for Schroeder.

All this had to surface before the trial could go on. Attorney Concannon repeated most of the facts he had presented to Dr. Woodward the day before. Then he said, "Now, I had asked you, Doctor, whether or not you had an opinion as to whether or not the defendant, Hans Schroeder, was suffering from any mental illness on November 2, 1966, and you've answered yes. And now I ask you, what is that opinion, and you may answer."

Defense Counsel objected, and the judge noted his objection.

"You asked me if he was suffering from any illness prior to November 2, 1969," began Dr. Woodward. "And I said that I had an opinion, yes. My opinion is that he was not suffering from any mental illness prior to November 2, 1966."

"I thought," interrupted Judge Collins, turning to the prosecution, that your question was whether he was suffering from a mental illness on November 2."

"I'll ask the question again, your Honour." Then, addressing the doctor once more, Mr. Concannon asked, "Was he suffering from a mental illness on November 2?"

After defense counsel's objection had been noted, Dr. Woodward said, "No, I don't believe he was."

"With respect to November 3, 4, 5 and 6," asked Mr. Concannon, "do you have an opinion as to whether or not the defendant was mentally capable of doing the voluntary act of confessing to a crime or admitting guilt?"

"Yes, I do," answered Dr. Woodward.

"And what is that opinion?"

"In my opinion, Mr. Schroeder was mentally capable of voluntarily confessing to a crime."

The questions and answers continued amidst a torrent of objections and exceptions from counsel for the defense. "Do you have an opinion," asked Mr. Concannon, "as to whether the admissions and statements made by the defendant, to which I've just alluded, were the products of a rational intellect?"

"Yes."

"And what is that opinion?"

"In my opinion, the confessions were the product of a voluntary intellect."

"Would you please give us the reasons for that opinion."

"Well, of course, the reasons for giving that opinion involve, er! my review of his Bridgewater record, where he was committed after arraignment for a determination as to his competency to stand trial. Also, the prior history that has been, I think, introduced. There has been so much confusion in my mind -"

"You have to confine yourself to what is now in the record in this hearing before you," interrupted the judge. "Do you have an opinion as to whether the statements and acts of this defendant on November 3, 4, 5 and 6 were the product of a rational intellect?"

"Yes, your Honour, I do. In my opinion, I believe they were the products of a rational intellect, and I have based my opinion on the facts in the medical history and the facts assumed in the question put to me."

It was defense counsel's turn to question Dr. Woodward. "When did you become a psychiatrist, Dr. Woodward?" asked Piscitelli.

"I completed my residency in psychiatry in 1955, and I would consider that I became a psychiatrist at that time."

"You took your boards at that time?"

"I took the boards in 1958, passed them."

"What are the boards?"

"They are, they are given by the American College of Psychiatry and Neurology, and they are a series of examinations, verbal and - well, verbal actually at the time I took them - in which you are asked to review the clinical cases, asked questions about the history and so forth of psychiatry. It's an attempt by the American Board to establish minimum standards for the practice of psychiatry."

"Then you take a two or three day examination and, if you pass, you become a psychiatrist, or you are certified. Is that correct?"

"If you pass you become a diplomate of the American Board of Psychiatry and Neurology. I consider that I was already a psychiatrist on July 1, 1955."

"You consider that a person who doesn't even take his boards can still be considered a psychiatrist. Is that correct?"

"Yes."

"Or can at least consider himself a psychiatrist?"

"Yes, I think he can be considered a psychiatrist."

"And you've been employed by the Commonwealth of Massachusetts now for some length of time, have you?"

"One year in my capacity as the Judge of the Brockton District — excuse me, your Honour."

"A Freudian slip," said attorney Piscitelli, smiling.

"Delusions of grandeur," added Dr. Woodward wryly. "I served as psychiatrist of the Brockton District Court. In all, I've been employed in various capacities for the Commonwealth of Massachusetts for over ten years."

"And I take it that you see many, many people in the course of your psychiatrist practice, do you not, Doctor?"

"That is correct."

"And you have to evaluate their mental conditions, right?" "That's correct."

"How many people do you think you've seen, would you say, in the last ten years for purposes of evaluation?"

"Thousands."

"Thousands. And it's fair to say that what you do is you sit down and talk to them and ask them questions,

I suppose, about their background and history and so forth, in an effort to evaluate their condition."

"Usually."

"But isn't that the normal procedure you use?"

"That's the usual procedure I employ."

"Okay. It's fair to say, Doctor, that you use that procedure because it's best to talk to the man you're going to evaluate and look at him and examine him really close. Right?"

"It's usually necessary to look at the man that you're reporting on."

"Right. And it's fair to say that in ninety-nine and forty-four one-hundredths percent of the cases, you have, in fact, seen them prior to evaluation."

"I would say it's more like ninety eight percent."

"All right. But that would afford the best possible opportunity to give an evaluation and diagnosis of the condition, right? When you see the man and eyeball him."

"Usually is, yes. Usually is possible."

"And it helps, Doctor, does it not, to see his demeanour and appearance, and the manner in which he speaks, whether he is faltering or hesitating or just what, right?"

"If I'm making an assessment -"

"Please answer -," interrupted counsel for the defense.

"- at a particular time, it's best to see him at that time, yes."

"Okay. When did you first see Hans Schroeder to form an opinion that you've made here, given here today, Doctor?"

"Of course, I've not seen Mr. Schroeder in a - in consultation."

"What you mean, Doctor Woodward, is that you've never once spoken to this man for the purpose of consultation, right? To determine his psychiatric competence back in November 1966. Is that correct?'

"That's true."

7

I didn't so much mind Woodward's opinions or Concannon's confidence. What upset me was the fact he called me a bus-driver in Wiesbaden. I was more than that. I made things with my hands. I fashioned toys. They were the most beautiful toys you could imagine. Everyone loved them. Katarina loved them most of all. But I am jumping ahead of my story.

Let me start at Munich. Yes, the city was full of memories and pain from the moment the train pulled up at the Haupt Bahnhof. The station was barely recognizable for the marvellous structure it had once been, built a hundred years ago from the plans of Friedrich Burklein. A web of scaffolding enfolded almost every wall left standing after the bombs. As I hoisted my canvas bag over my shoulders and stepped into the Bayerstrasse, I felt a fleeting hint of what Munich had been through. But I also felt overcome with self-pity and uncertainty, and soon the city's troubles receded into the distance.

It soon occurred to me that the city had surrendered itself to an army of masons, bricklayers, and sundry laborers. They seemed everywhere. But the laborers looked grim, there was no joy in the faces of this army. I didn't see a single man smile. As I crossed the Karlsplatz and drew up to the badly damaged Michaelskirche, I felt the worm of hopelessness and anger burrowing deeper into my mind. Most of the walls of this exquisite Renaissance church were in the process of being slowly and painstakingly restored. But one look through an open door told me that all the statues and the awesome vaults were gone. It was about the same with the Frauenkirche further down the street. The beautiful stained glass windows were gone. Only the old tombstones on the outer walls seemed to have escaped.

At the Marienplatz, the famous beer-house known as 'Zum bayerischen Donisl' had disappeared. Like the stained glass windows I loved, the boisterous music that reverberated through the place had vanished into the wind and the dust. But like the tombstones of the Frauenkirche, there still stood the marble Mariensaule in the middle of the square. At the corners of the bronze figure of the Virgin, four winged genii, four survivors, stood contending against Plague, War, Famine and Heresy. I felt I could laugh, but my upbringing prevented me from causing offence to the people walking around.

The Peterskirche was in ruins, so was the Heiliggeistkirche. I circled aimlessly through the centre of the city. The life on the streets was utterly new to me, and yet I paid no attention to it. I was looking for the past, my own and that of my fellow Germans. It lay here and there in broken chunks, in the dust, perhaps even in faraway museums, yearning for the Nile like Nefertiti.

Like the genii around the Virgin's statue, the Wittelsbach Fountain in the Maximiliansplatz stood out like a symbol more comical than solemn. The maiden riding, the water-bull, the boy on the shattered water-horse. What lived on in them seemed to be the destruction man and nature heaped on all things, certainly not the breath of life. Tired and confused, I found a single church, that of the Holy Trinity on one side of the Pfandhausstrasse, that appeared totally intact. I walked in, sat down, and continued to feel sorry for myself.

It would be so easy, I thought, to remain a prisoner of my own dissatisfactions, to give in without a fight. Then my head began to throb, and the pain that had begun only in my thoughts suddenly seized my neck, my shoulders, and began to creep down my back.

I must have passed out or something. A tide of voices breaking forth in song suddenly woke me up with a start. I think it was the cathedral choir starting to practice. The Opera House steps on which I had spent so many hours flashed through my mind. In earlier times, I would've let my thoughts ride the music to the clouds. Instead, I picked up my bag and scrambled for one of the doors through which faint street sounds were drifting in. It was almost as if the music drove me into the streets.

Outside, it was cool and dark. Once more, I started down the Pfandhaustrasse in the general direction of the Hauptpost on Maximilian-Strasse. Then, remembering the Hofbrauhaus in the Platzl, I quickly turned into one of the side streets beyond the ruined post office.

It was in the beer house that, for the first time, I think I came face to face with American service-men. I may have seen them elsewhere too. Here, there was no way you could mistake or avoid them. The deafening noise, the glow of the yellow lamps, and the fact that virtually all German males seemed to have been banished from the hall, these made it difficult to relate to the Americans with warmth or understanding. It came as something of a shock to me to realize that, of course, there were Germans in the hall. But these were women. The attention they lavished on their companions or patrons was nothing short of shameless. To this day I have not been able to forgive them.

They were crude imitations, cracked, peeling, deformed, not the women I knew in my youth. Not the women whose devotion and admiration made the German male eager to take on the gods themselves. I think I grew hopelessly drunk as the night wore on. My anger and resentment over German girls being caressed and fondled by the victors soon changed into an unbearable pain. They made it look so easy for these men. It was different in the Russian camp, with women like Tulla. There was no room for forgiveness here. These women were out to destroy something in me. They had destroyed my father, now they were out to destroy me.

I spent a long time looking for a spot which held for me my most enduring image of my father. He had moved to Munich in 1935, lured by a minor clerical position in the Bavarian State Library on the beautiful Ludwigstrasse. He had leanings towards the Social Democrats and held the Nazis in low esteem. When he found out that I had joined the Hitler Jugend he was sad and angry. He thought I was crazy to be moving with the hysterical surge of what he called the tragic generation. I thought it was a good way to teach him a lesson, faint-hearted that he was, unwilling to support the nation embarking on what we then believed to be Germany's greatest hour.

The place I was looking for was the balcony of a synagogue not far from the Weinstadel. Our Hitler Jugend group climbed upon the roof of the synagogue one afternoon. We were to fix a swastika flag to its steeple. I and two others had the flag. I happened to look down, and there, in the crowd below, watching us, was my father. Father was too afraid to say anything. He just looked at me and shook his head, slowly and sadly. In his own way, I suppose he was a fine man, somewhat weak. I still remember him that way. But I never found the synagogue.

I thought about the future as I sat on my bed in a cheap rooming house near the centre of town. Munich depressed me. My money was running out. Somehow I lacked the energy to go looking for a job. There were agencies galore, each with the shadow of an uniformed American serviceman hovering over it. The American presence was so total in Munich that the city gradually began to resemble another prison for me. I didn't need to be reminded how vastly different it all was from Yercevo. It still felt like a prison to me.

I never planned my freedom. I had no real sense of what to do from one moment to the other. I began to think of my mother one evening, somewhat casually, not with any sense of deep affection. I suddenly made up my mind to return to Wiesbaden. Perhaps I'd be able to make a fresh start there.

My heart grew heavy at seeing the broken Haupt Bahnhof once more. But only for a moment or so. As the train sped through the countryside, my heart ached as I felt more and more overwhelmed by the beauty of the land. It took my breath away. It had healed so quickly. As I sat entranced by the window, it was easy to forget there had ever been a war. But the illusion soon left me, almost as soon as I took a deep breath and looked inside the carriage for someone to share my pleasure with. I was deeply disappointed as I realized that my half dozen fellow passengers were all wearing uniforms of the United States Air Force. As my eyes met those of the American sitting directly in front of me, the stranger smiled and nodded. I felt uneasy about not responding in some way or the other. So I smiled faintly and nodded my head up and down several times. Later, I felt my ears grow hot as I began to feel more and more of a fool.

I got off at the Wiesbaden railway station and started walking up Nicolasstrasse in the direction of the Town Hall. If the buildings along the road looked somewhat neglected and tired, the neat rows of trees and the spotless gardens soon blew away my misgivings. There was something solid and respectable about the town, something of a quiet, confident pride. I liked the feel of it. It sat well with my sense of tradition and propriety.

The sun was strong. My canvas bag was heavy with some cheap novels I had bought off the sidewalk in Munich. At the junction of Bahnhofstrasse and Rheinstrasse, I stopped under a large tree right in front of the post office. I laid my bag on the ground and stretched myself. As I looked up at the twisted branches over my head, I felt the diffused light of the bright sun filtering through the leaves isolating me from my surroundings and filling me with a sense of profound calm. Yes, Wiesbaden would be all right to begin afresh. My spirit grew light and soared. I heaved the bag over my shoulders once more. I wanted to get back into the sun. There was a sensuous excitement in the sun's rays that I had all but forgotten in Russia.

A policeman stood in my way as I crossed Friedrichstrasse and caught sight of the Town Hall. At first, the policeman's presence annoyed me. I wasn't sure whether to look the man straight in the face or walk around him, pretending I hadn't even noticed him. I soon realized the policeman was merely standing in front of the town's police station, right at the bottom of the steps in fact. I felt better about the encounter then.

The policeman was looking in my direction. Our eyes met and the man asked me if I was new in town. His voice was warm and friendly. I said I was, adding that I was looking for work.

"Should be able to find something here," said the policeman. "Enquire at the stores on the Webergasse. Might also try some of the smaller places on the Burgstrasse. Then there are the hotels."

I walked along the street a little longer, mindful of the fact that the policeman had not suggested I try the fashionable stores along the Wilhelmstrasse. The suggestion about trying the hotels seemed to have been thrown in almost as an afterthought.

For the first time in years, I began to feel terribly self-conscious about my appearance. My fingers strayed to my face. Perhaps it was my beard. I looked down at my rumpled clothes, the same ones I had put on at Moscow airport, an official farewell gift from the

Russians. It had to be my clothes, I concluded. Perhaps that was why I had unconsciously chosen to walk along the Nicolasstrasse rather than the Kaiserstrasse upon leaving the railway station. There seemed no other reason to avoid the avenues I loved. I knew quite well that the Kaiserstrasse led to the Wilhelmstrasse. From the steps of the red sandstone railway station I could see many of the grand and elegant buildings on the street. And yet, my feet led me to the less imposing Nicolasstrasse.

I left the policeman behind and stopped once more in front of the Town Hall. I remembered every nook and cranny of that building. I made a mental note to come back and climb those majestic steps and sit under the lofty arches, much as I used to do in front of Schiller's statue. For the time being, I had to move on.

I passed the old castle and the Gothic church and decided it was time to eat something. I was in no mood just then to start searching for my mother. I scanned the grounds of the Kaiser-Friedrich-Bad. Seeing the way the people were dressed, and the baggage they carried, as they walked up and down the marble steps of the bath-house, I knew it was business as usual. I also knew there was nothing there that I could eat. No stalls, no vendors. Only the unhurried traffic winding along the garden paths. Without intending to, I took a right turn and stumbled into the Webergasse.

I stood in front of the glistening store windows and took another note of my appearance. I turned to look at the others along the street. The women all looked young, lean, and elegant. The men wore expensive suits or American uniforms. I laughed to think that anyone along this stretch would be mad enough to offer me a job. The policeman was probably mocking me when he mentioned the Webergasse.

Wandering through Munich, I had often passed large, expensive stores. Somehow, I didn't feel inclined to give those places a second look. I was still carrying a leaden feeling at the back of my mind which kept my thoughts pinned to the snow-clad desolation of my seven years in Siberia. Wiesbaden led me to believe I was perhaps beginning to break free. I was feeling a renewed interest in the present, the moment at hand. So it was that I stood for a long time staring at the rich vests and blue and black gowns glittering in Bacharach's display windows until they seemed to fill out with the flesh of beautiful women and quivered before my eyes.

A group of giggling schoolgirls passed by. Their presence shook me out of my trance. I moved along. There would be time here for new friendships, I told myself. Wiesbaden was less frenetic, less savaged, than Munich. I could see many years of my life in this town. What a fool I was to leave.

On the other side of the street, the linen store of Emma Kluke caught my eyes. I crossed the street to take a closer look at the store front. Through the large glass window, I saw a riot of colours in bed and table linen, and the latest styles in fancy tea and luncheon sets. But what stirred me most was something on display closest to the street. A most exquisite collection of handworked silk underwear. As I stared in curiosity at the delicate embroidery and the fine laces, I noticed through a corner of my eyes that the schoolgirls who had passed me in front of Bacharach's were now approaching Emma Kluke's shop. I felt confused and embarrassed at what the girls might think of me. I wheeled around quickly and returned to the other side of the street. There, in front of me, lay a store dedicated for as long as I could remember to the noble art of letter-writing. It was called Holstinsky's.

I stood in front of the open door and stared at the expensive boxes of stationery, delicate Viennese bronzes, leather bookmarks and covers, and every conceivable object for the writing table. Tears came to my eyes as I thought of letters and realized how long I had been shut away from my fellow Germans. I hadn't received a single letter in seven years.

I kept on walking and finally came to a stop in front of a child's wonderland. It was Wiegel and Company. I once believed, and still do, that it was the greatest toy store in the world. I found an electric train running behind the glass window. It was complete with signals, engines, railway platforms, marshalling yards, cabooses, and even boxcars. I was so engrossed in the train that I didn't notice a middle-aged man operating the system from one side. It was probably the light reflecting off the glass that prevented me from seeing Hans Wiegel. I forget how long I had been standing there. I guess I just kept standing there long after Hans had stopped working the signals and the train had stopped. I was transfixed to the spot, my feet refused to move. I was awakened from my reverie by a hand resting gently on my shoulder. It was Hans. I looked into his kind eyes, startled.

"Hello," said Hans.

"Hello, I was admiring the train."

"It's beautiful, isn't it?" asked Hans. "I love it too."

"Yes," I said.

"Are you new in town?" 'Yes," I answered again. "Where are you from?"

Normally, I would've resisted answering that question. But Hans' gentle voice and the gentle touch of his hand were quite disarming. "Seven days in Munich," I said, "and seven years in Siberia." I felt embarrassed as I blurted out, "I'm looking for a job in Wiesbaden."

Hans looked at me intently for a moment or two before speaking. "I think I can find you a job," he said.

"Where?" I asked excitedly.

"Right here in my store," he said. With his hand encircling my shoulder, Hans led me quietly through the door.

8

My name is Dr. Robert Ross Mezer. My office is 330 Dartmouth Street in Boston. I graduated from Boston Latin School in 1939, received my A.B. degree from Harvard in 1942, my M.D. degree from Tufts Medical School in 1945. I interned for a year at Boston City Hospital from 1945 to 1946. I then undertook psychiatric residency training first at the Bedford and Cushing Veterans Hospitals between 1946 and 1948. Then further residency training at the Boston Psychopathic Hospital from 1948 to 1949. It's now known as the Massachusetts Mental Health Center. Since 1949, I have been in private practice of psychiatry in Boston. I'm a diplomate of the American Board of Medical Examiners since 1946 and certified by the American Board of Psychiatry and Neurology as a specialist in psychiatry, having been so certified in 1951. I've held staff positions at the Massachusetts Mental Health Center as a Senior Psychiatrist between 1949 and 1956. From 1956 to 1959, I was Clinical Director of the Parole Clinic, Commonwealth of Massachusetts. The Clinic is part of the Division of Legal Medicine, Department of Mental Health, Commonwealth of Massachusetts. From 1959 to 1960, I was Coordinator of the Psychiatry Training Programme at the Law-Medicine Research Institute. I've had several teaching affiliations at Harvard Medical School, an Instructor from 1949 to

1959. Also, Visiting Instructor in Psychiatry from 1951 to 1959 at the Massachusetts General Hospital School of Nursing. At Boston University, I held a joint appointment as Assistant Professor of Legal Psychiatry at the Law School and as Assistant Professor of Psychiatry at the Medical School. I have published several articles which have appeared in both psychiatric and legal journals. I published a textbook in psychiatry which is presently in its fourth edition. It is used in the teaching of medical students, nurses, psychologists, social workers, and residents undergoing their psychiatric training. The book has been published in several foreign countries. I'm a member of several professional societies, a fellow of the American Psychiatric Association, former member of their Committee on Law and Psychiatry, and councillor of the Massachusetts Medical Society. I'm a former member of their Committee on Mental Health. I'm a member of the Norfolk District Medical Society wherein I'm chairman of their Committee on Mental Health. I'm a member of the National Council on Crime and Delinquency and several other professional organizations. I'm listed in several directories, including American Men of Medicine, Directory of Medical Specialists, and Who's Who in the East.

I first saw Hans Schroeder at the Bridgewater State Hospital on November 11, 1966. I saw him again on November 22, on May 26, 1967, September 16, 1967, February 14, 1968, March 2, 1968, January 9, 1973, and September 13, 1973. At the time when I saw him, he was suffering from a psychotic depressive reaction. Perhaps I should define depression first.

Depression is a feeling of sadness, and some depressive reactions are perfectly normal. We receive a disappointment, an unfavourable outcome in some venture, lose a relative. It's quite normal to be depressed. That's normal depressive reaction. An abnormal depressive reaction is one which lasts a long period of time. People get over normal depressive reactions in a day, a week, a month. Depressive reactions tend to settle in, sometimes for weeks, months, even years. A normal depressive reaction is differentiated from an abnormal depressive reaction in terms of its severity. It is seldom indeed that a normal depressive reaction leads a person to suicide, to suicidal attempts or threats. It's usually a self-contained type of depressive feeling. A psychotic depressive reaction, on the other hand, frequently leads a person to feel suicidal. Such persons often make attempts to commit suicide, and a substantial number eventually succeed in killing themselves. In addition to that, in a normal depressive reaction the physiological and physical aspects are apt to be minimal and not long-lasting. In the abnormal depressive reactions, these physical aspects tend to be severe as well as long-lasting. These physical reactions can involve headaches, gastrointestinal disturbances, diarrhoea, constipation, belching, vomiting, and things of that nature. Frequent urination is also often involved. Sometimes it's so severe the person is incontinent of urine and faeces and loses his urine and faeces. In addition, the person experiences extreme agitation, which is normally absent in normal reactive depression.

While these are a few elements that differentiate the field of depression, we also have to differentiate between the normal and the psychotic. Psychosis is a major, serious and severe mental illness in which the subject loses contact with reality. A person is frequently not responsible for his behaviour while in the psychotic phase of various types of mental illness. The psychoses, in turn, are divided into organic psychoses such as organic brain diseases and psychological impairments which accompany old age and arterial sclerosis. There are functional psychoses such as schizophrenia or manic-depressive, illnesses in which there is nothing the matter with the brain, physically or organically, but the individual is seriously disturbed psychologically.

The psychotic depressive reaction that I have diagnosed Mr. Schroeder as having at the time when I saw him is this severe, serious type, a major mental illness in which depression is characterized by powerful physical and physiological aspects with suicide a prominent part of it. He was showing disturbances in sleep, disturbances in gastrointestinal functioning, disturbances in his ability to maintain contact with reality. In my opinion, there were also disturbances in his responsibility for his behaviour.

Mr. Schroeder was referred for psychiatric observation by his attorney in order to evaluate his competency to stand trial and his mental state at the time of the crimes he is accused of committing, the killings of his wife, Eva, and his daughter, Katarina. At the time, Mr. Schroeder gave his chief complaints as depression, crying spells, inability to eat and sleep, tension and anxiety, agitation, confusion, and loss of memory.

The details of his past history as far as I could gather are as follows. Born in Wiesbaden in 1921. Had the usual childhood diseases. In 1946 he had an appendectomy while a prisoner of war in a Russian prison camp. He also had a throat operation that same year. He had malaria several times between 1945 and 1947. He may also have had either typhus or typhoid fever. He was involved in two accidents as a bus driver, sustaining a concussion in 1955. Back in 1952, he suffered concussion plus injuries to his back and neck. He had an eighth grade education in Germany plus three years of trade school where he learned selling, buying, and office procedures. In March 1938, at the age of seventeen he entered the service of the German army. In September 1944, he was captured by the Russians and sent to a Russian prison camp in Siberia.

In America, to which he came in 1956 with his wife and daughter, Katarina, Mr. Schroeder worked as a dishwasher for a few months, in a shoe factory for eighteen months, as a salesman for Woolworth's in Boston and Middleboro for three years. From August 1961 to September 1966, he worked at Capital Appliance Center of Plymouth as a manager earning $125.00 per week.

In 1966, his mother was sixty two years old, living and well. She came to America on her own in 1953, her husband having disappeared just before the start of the war. There is no family history of mental illness or serious physical disability. Nor is there any family history of criminality. I enquired about previous criminal record and found that Mr. Schroeder had no such record whatsoever. In fact, he was an outstanding member of the community. He served as president of the Middlesex Merchants' Bowling League, and vice-president of the local Parent-Teachers Association. Mr. Schroeder had no previous record of psychiatric hospitalization and had not consulted a psychiatrist prior to the onset of the present illness.

The history of his present illness has some salient points. On February 13, 1966, his wife took an overdose of barbiturates in a suicide attempt. She was admitted to the Chalmers Hospital in a comatose condition, and then removed to the Taunton State Hospital in March for further treatment of her mental condition. She received medication and was discharged in May of 1966.

It was during the period when his wife was in hospital that Mr. Schroeder began to experience depression himself. He was upset when he found his wife lying in a coma on the floor after her suicide attempt. He himself called the doctor and had her admitted to the hospital. While she remained in hospital, he had to stay home to care for the four children. He had to stay away from work. The unpaid bills piled up. During the three months when his wife lay in the hospital, he felt financially devastated. Eventually he had to take a leave of absence from his job at Capital Appliance Center, and this made him more tense, more worried, and more depressed. Even after Mrs. Schroeder was released from the hospital, she was unable to resume her household functions. She wasn't able to take care of the house and children. Mr. Schroeder couldn't therefore return to work on a full-time basis. The family slid further and further into debt. Mr. Schroeder switched jobs in late September and went to work for the Lahey Gas Company.

The idea was to bring in more money for the family. But he continued to be in a very depressed, tense, and agitated state of mind. That was the way he was at the time when the crimes occurred. He had several drinks of cognac and beer before he arrived home. His wife gave him a jigger glass of anisette. Mr. Schroeder still didn't feel good. He remained depressed. His head hurt. He felt drowsy and confused. He lay down on his bed and everything seemed to be turning around him. He thought he heard one of the children cry. He recalls kneeling beside Chris's bed, feeling sick and sweating profusely.

The next thing he remembered is awakening to hear a buzzer ringing, and finding that it was broad daylight. He found himself kneeling at his son, Chris's, bed. He discovered his wife dead in her bedroom. Katarina was dead too. He was scared, confused, couldn't understand what had happened. He got the other children dressed and into the car. He took his wife's pills, some aspirin tablets, and a bottle of cognac. He kept popping pills in his mouth and drank as he drove around with the children. He thinks he must have left the children off in a motel, but he had only a dim recollection of this. He recalls vomiting and being incontinent of both urine and faeces. In the midst of his confused state, he heard the car radio announce that Hans Schroeder had killed his wife and daughter. He couldn't believe what he was hearing. He got out of the car, walked over to some hunters. He was dazed, confused, depressed, crying, and asked the hunters to call the police.

His deep depression continued throughout the time when I was examining him. He was unable to recall exactly what had happened. He couldn't figure out why. He cried throughout the psychiatric examination. His stomach was upset. He belched repeatedly and said he felt like vomiting. He was agitated and tense, had difficulty in sitting quietly, paced the floor, and pulled his hair. All this while I was talking to him. He complained of a headache, of dizziness and blurred vision. He told me he was unable to sleep and that he had lost his appetite. I found him mildly disoriented. He had suicidal thoughts and ideas which he expressed freely to me. I could elicit no hallucinations at the time when I saw him, although he described a noise in his head that might have been a hallucination. He described it as the murmuring of a seashell held to the ear. He didn't describe any actual voices or imaginary noises. Over and over, he kept expressing disbelief that he had killed his wife and daughter as he had been told that he had, and wondered why he would ever do such a thing. His memory for remote events appeared to be intact. He remembered events in the distant past, but he had no memory for the events of the crime. His memory for events after the crime was confused and inexact. He wasn't, for example, sure where and when he had left the children off.

I evaluated his intelligence and found he was of at least average intelligence. I arrived at a diagnosis of psychotic depressive reaction. There is hope that with proper psychiatric treatment Mr. Schroeder will be able to recover from this condition in time.

Given the same set of facts, several psychiatrists may differ on a diagnosis. In the present case, the Bridgewater State Hospital report concerning Mr. Schroeder states that he remembers nothing from the time of the offense and can recollect nothing in regard to it. Such confusion and lack of memory is perfectly consistent with a diagnosis of psychotic depressive reaction. The Bridgewater report points out that, on admission, he was extremely depressed and crying and was unable to give any account of the details of the crime. He states he remembers nothing, even to being arrested in Connecticut. When told the facts about his charges, he simply expressed his disbelief and could not understand what motives he may have had at the time. There is also a reference here to a sea shell murmur in his head. The pains are constant in the area of the right frontal lobe. He still has periods when he cannot orient himself and periods of minor blackouts. He is able to compose himself and pull himself out of his slumps, but his vision often continues to remain cloudy and vague.

According to the report, he ate supper and went to bed, requesting Eva to put a pan next to his bed in case he vomited. As he lay on the bed, he said it was like being on a carousel, everything went round and round. The next memory he has is waking up, freezing, in a deep wood in his car, having soiled himself and covered with vomit, listening to a news broadcast which said that the fugitive, Hans Schroeder, having killed his wife and oldest daughter, and taking the remaining children, was escaping towards the Canadian border. Horrified and shocked by this news, he got out of the car and, surprisingly, found himself drunk, something that hadn't happened to him before. He found two bottles of vodka in the car. Totally confused as to what had happened to him, and the car being out of gas, he started running through the woods. He heard the sound of shooting in the distance and followed the sound until he ran into two hunters. To them, he said, "Take me, I'm Hans Schroeder, the murderer." They

stared at him in disbelief and decided to call the police. He was subsequently sent to Bridgewater and to
this date denies any memory of what went on.

If the court wants to know my opinion about the
inception of Mr. Schroeder's psychotic depressive reaction, I would say that he experienced several rejections during a month or so prior to November 1966
and a week prior to the date in question. I feel these
rejections precipitated the psychotic depressive reaction. The neurotic depressive reaction had been going
on ever since his wife made those suicide attempts.
That's when the bills began to pile up and he had to
stay home from work to take care of his family. Finally,
his rejection by Mrs. Peggy Constanza precipitated the
psychotic depressive reaction. Such reaction usually
comes on gradually and then builds up. Then, some
major stressful event comes along as the proverbial
straw that breaks the camel's back. That precipitates
the psychotic depressive reaction.

Yes, even a trivial incident can precipitate a psychotic depressive reaction, but only if that trivial incident falls like a seed on fertile soil. In other words,
if the individual has been subjected to stresses and
strains, disappointments and difficulties, such that when
the trivial thing happens he is almost gone, then that
trivial incident may tip him over. A person with normal
strengths and normal capacity, on the other hand, can
take such a trivial event in stride. It would not precipitate
a psychotic depressive reaction in such a person. Hans
Schroeder was being overwhelmed by the reality situation of his wife being ill and having to go to a mental
hospital. He had to take care of the children, he couldn't
work, the debts piled up. A conscientious person, an

honorable person, a community leader, all this was very hard for him to take. The house deteriorated. With all this turmoil inside, the house was nowhere as clean as it would usually be. All these things weighed down on him seriously. Then, somewhere in his mind, he developed this delusion, this infatuation for Mrs. Constanza. It didn't have any reality to it, but it was one of the last straws he was grasping at before he went under. This prop was taken away from him by Mrs. Constanza's rejection. The woman thought he was crazy. She had no interest in him. I think he cracked when he had this last vestige of hope taken away from him. There may have been other things in addition, that led to the final dissolution. He may have been under pressure that weekend or the day of the event because of sickness in the family or some other reason. For me as a therapist, the details of such events are not that important. What is important is that he had a major psychotic episode. And this interfered substantially with his ability to conform to the requirements of the law at the time in question. That is, if he did in fact commit these crimes. If he did not, the discovery of his wife and daughter being dead certainly made him go over the edge and interfered with his capacity to be rational from then on. Certainly, his behavior has no element of rationality to it as he took the kids and drank as he drove, and took pills and left the kids somewhere he didn't exactly know where. He was confused, hears the announcement on the radio, gets out of the car with a blanket over his head covered with faeces and vomit, belching and crying, and hysterical and upset. Any statement of guilt that he might then make to the police or others cannot be taken to be a rational statement.

9

⮜⮜⮜⮜⮜⮜⮜⮜⮜⮜

I met Eva as she was staring at the shop window one evening in spring. Hans had allowed me to fill the display with about three dozen animals I had painstakingly carved out of wood during the past two or three months. They looked nice in the window, with a wooded forest, a barn, and an open field providing the right background for the cattle, the sheep, the elephants, lions, and giraffes. I had seen many passersby stop and look at the figures and I knew they appreciated my work even though they didn't know who I was.

There was something else that drew me to Eva. Not the fact that there was obvious pleasure in her face when she saw my animals. Rather, it was a look of utter disbelief, of a childlike wonder, that attracted my attention. I felt I had to go outside and introduce myself. I think they were playing Mozart in the park that evening. There was a strange magic in the air as I stepped outside and stood beside Eva. I told her I had carved the animals myself and asked if she liked them. She looked startled and confused, and said, "Yes, yes," as she smiled and started to walk away. The music played on, but I began to feel an immense sense of loss.

My mother remarked how distracted I looked when I went to take her to church the following Sunday.

"It is spring time, my son," she told me. "I think you might be in love." Impossible as it sounded to me then, I realized how correct she was when I caught sight of Eva the following week. I suppose I must have been watching out for her. But there she was, walking somewhat slowly, casting a sideways glance at the store window as she walked by. This time I confronted her directly, standing in her way, and introducing myself.

It was a beautiful spring and an even more wondrous summer. Eva and I were in love. She held a clerical position in Biebrich Palace, the summer residence of the Duke of Nassau. Soon we knew every tree, every flower on the Biebrich riverside promenade by heart. We practically lived there. Another spot we loved was the walk through the lovely Nerotal which took us to the Neroberg. We held hands in the twilight as we stared at the city and the Rhine valley stretched out below us and tried to pick out familiar landmarks. As it grew dark, we found ourselves in the shadows, locked in embrace, much like the figures I remembered from my childhood.

It was in this kind of a communion with nature that we found our greatest joy. That and the solidity of the city of Wiesbaden, its exquisite gabled buildings, its sense of timelessness. Of course, we never thought of its fragility. A few well-placed American bombs would have sent everything crashing to hell. The music would've stopped and the baths choked with debris.

Hans Wiegel was too kind to me. I knew I would never get rich working for him, but it never occurred to me to leave him and look for something more promising elsewhere. Perhaps it was the very nature of the work that held me captive. The toys that I shaped out of wood, the figures I moulded out of clay, all these were pleasurable experiences by themselves. More importantly, they kept me close to children and made me feel like a child. I must admit there was a little pain too. It came whenever I felt haunted by the memory of Tulla. It didn't take long for the love I had for Eva to set me free from painful memories and the spell of ghosts from the past. I realize today it was not freedom, simply a parole. Less than a year later, we were married in St. Boniface's Church. It was not a big wedding. We were all poor in those days. Wiesbaden was still something of a sleepy town in nineteen forty nine. A small wedding was not unusual, and it was good enough for us.

We found two small rooms on a steep and narrow street in the Bergkirchen area. We bought our bread, our sausages and groceries within a minute's walk from where we lived. I could never imagine we'd ever be happier than we were then.

The only problem was the time it took Eva to travel to her job in the Biebrich Palace. It was proving to be too much for her. She would be exhausted when she returned home each evening. I quickly made up my mind one day late that summer. She had to find another job. Things were not right in our little home.

Mr. Wiegel knew a lot of Americans. Within a matter of days he had found Eva a job as a cashier at the American Servicemen's Club. Now it took her less than half an hour to get to work. I began to feel more at ease, more relaxed than I had been a few weeks ago. Once more, our modest home began to sparkle like a diamond, or so Mother assured me.

Eva liked her job at the club. It was not demanding at all, the people were friendly and the pay was good. We saved up enough money to go to Berlin the following summer. Unfortunately, it wasn't a very happy experience. While in Berlin, I seemed to come face to face with a part of myself I had almost forgotten. They seemed to have pierced Berlin through the heart and then ground it to dust. It was in the dust that I found what I had once been, proud, defiant, a creature from the heavens. I found Berlin humiliating.

When I returned to Wiesbaden that August, I began to look at our conquerors in a different way. Earlier, I felt nothing. There was no sense of anger, no sense of wonder. But all that changed.

There were many girls in Wiesbaden who still went out with Germans. But many had left their parents, their homes, and now lived in apartments which their American boy friends had rented for them. The Americans were quite businesslike when they approached German families, and offered them cigarettes or money in return for one room. Then their German girls would move into this room. When the American went back home, the German girl tried to meet another before she had to move out of the single room. I once thought nothing of German girls waiting outside the American barracks. Now I felt differently.

Many women of my mother's generation went to work for the Americans washing dishes or waiting at tables. This was one way they could get food or money for themselves or their children. I found Mother and her friends had a sad name for the girls waiting for the American soldiers at the barracks doors. They called them Ruinenmauschen, or Ruin-mice, after the poor little mice which once lived in the ruins of bombed houses in many German cities, feeding perhaps on the bodies which still lay underneath, or on buried food, growing fat on the corpse of a mangled Germany. I only felt pity for these German women, for they were not evil. Only weak, innocent little things who needed a roof over their heads and food to live. Hans Wiegel stunned me one day with a comment about these girls. "We stood up for six years against the whole world," he said, "but now our women lie down in five minutes."

It was sometime before the birth of Katarina that I remember Eva bringing home American magazines and papers in quantities much larger than she had brought before. They never interested me much. But now I could hardly move from one room to the other, from the kitchen to the bathroom, without finding one such magazine staring me in the face. In time, she began to dream aloud about going to America. She was pregnant, and I thought it was part of her somewhat sentimental behavior to dream about far away places. So, even though I refused to listen to her, I could not bring myself to be angry with her. But I must admit she was beginning to wear me out.

I think this was the time when I first became aware of Harry. At the start of our friendship, I didn't quite know whether he was a German or an American. He spoke both languages fluently. But sometimes he claimed he was born in Dresden, and on other occasions he would have us believe he was born of American missionary parents in Africa. When I told him about Eva's dreams of moving to America he just laughed. It was a laughter placed somewhere between disbelief and scorn.

"Women are content to dream," he said, "but it is men who must act." I never knew what to make of statements like that, especially since there were times when he couldn't help singing the praises of America's power, the freedom of its institutions, and its wealth.

When he spoke of Germany, Harry was almost indistinguishable from Hans, Hans Wiegel that is. It was a glorious feeling to have around us in Wiesbaden so many symbols of Germany's greatness. "The refined build, the heathens destroy," he was fond of saying. It was from him that I began to believe that toymakers were indeed the architects of children's hearts. The dark side of this belief held my sense of frustration at never having had a chance to touch the heart of Tulla's child. Or maybe I had, but had no means of knowing it.

I was not going to take any chances when Eva's child was born. Hans — or was it Harry? — kept encouraging me to carve wooden birds and colour them with the rainbow, and little dirigibles trailing fancy ribbons while moored to the ceiling. When the child came, I was ready with dozens of little pieces, each a thing of beauty. I spent hours by Katarina's bed, watching her follow the colours under the ceiling and giggling when the wind stirred them to life.

Seeing my lack of enthusiasm for the subject, Eva had all but dropped the topic of travelling to America. But then Mother sprang a surprise on us. At the end of the first winter following Katarina's birth, she announced she was moving to America. Her papers had come through. It was quite a shock to me, since

I hadn't even known that she had ever completed an immigration application. "What's the use of staying on here any longer?" she asked. "All that we loved has turned to dust."

I didn't think she was correct in making that statement about Wiesbaden, but I never argued with her and saw no point in doing so now. Harry was unpredictably ecstatic over the news, but Mr. Wiegel grew distant and sullen over the next few weeks. "She could at least have discussed it with you or me," he said. "If everyone thought like her, who would be left in Germany but the mice?"

I am certain Hans Wiegel's references to mice had nothing to do with it. But soon afterwards I started carving figures of mice with a passion. I carved them scuttling across the floor on all fours. I carved them dancing on the streets during Gibber Kerb, quaffing goblets of wine at the Hochheim Wine Festival, and dancing on the Wilhelmstrasse during the summer fair. I dressed them up in the most beautiful fabrics which I gathered from Eva's leftovers after she had made Katarina's dresses.

Katarina loved the mice. The ones I made for her, I made specially large so she wouldn't swallow them accidentally. Before Mother left, she gave a name to each mouse in Katarina's collection of mice. Of course, she couldn't speak a word at the time. But before Katarina was three, she knew the names of each one of them. The mice were her pride and joy. Neighbors used to bring their house guests to our apartment in order to show off Katarina's collection of mice. Some of their praises were for me too, and it made me very happy.

Hans and I had a falling out of sorts one Christmas. It's still too painful for me to talk about it. But since others are stripping me naked in the courtroom, at least I should have the privilege of doing the same to myself. The truth is I caught Hans Wiegel in bed with Eva after the Christmas dinner at his house. I must have passed out shortly after the meal. The warmth of the fire in Hans's library might have had something to do with it. It was well past midnight when I woke up and went stumbling around the house and saw what I saw.

Hans said I was a fool with a fevered imagination. But he didn't try to dissuade me when I told him I would no longer work at the toyshop. I was out driving a schoolbus the very next week. Unfortunately, I was involved in a rather serious bus accident a few months later when I knocked up my head pretty badly. Nobody else was hurt, because there were no children in the bus at the time. I would never have been able to forgive myself if a single child had been hurt. I was without a job for weeks afterwards. Nobody wanted me in a job which demanded I drive a vehicle. Nobody wanted an ex-toymaker either.

I would meet Harry from time to time, especially in beer halls in the evening. He sounded very mysterious when he told me one day I should be thinking of leaving Wiesbaden. Maybe there was some wisdom in Eva's idea of going to America. After all, hadn't Mother been writing glowing letters about Massachusetts? "I'll drop by," said Harry, "and find out how Eva still feels about going."

I wasn't around when Harry dropped by. When I asked Eva one day about Harry's promised visit and the questions he was going to ask her, she promptly replied that there had never been any doubt in her mind that America would be an infinitely better place for us to move to, especially since Katarina was growing up and would soon need a good education to give her the right start in life. "What are we going to do once we are there?" I asked her. To which she replied, rightly I believe, that anything was better than waiting at home, hoping that a job would come by.

Harry never told me whether or not he ever went around to chat with Eva. But he was delighted when I told him about my conversation with her. "You should move at least for Katarina's sake," he said. "She'll be just like any other American kid. Nobody'll suspect she is German."

I think I was stunned by the remark, but I didn't show it.

10

ay it please the Court. Mr. Foreman, ladies and gentlemen, ladies and gentlemen of the jury. Hans Schroeder is accused of first degree murder. The penalty in this Commonwealth for first degree murder is death. And that is why you and I stand face to face here on this very lovely afternoon.

What I am about to say is not evidence. If in the course of my stating or making arguments to you, I say something inaccurately or not as you recall it, then please disregard what I say. Because it's your collective memory which will govern, not mine, that is, attorney Piscitelli's. But I will not do so intentionally.

Now you are the judges of the facts. His Honour will give you in this case the law which is to be applied to the facts that you find. And facts simply mean truth. You are to return a verdict. The verdict is simply two Latin words, veritas and dictum, which means to speak the truth. And that is what your verdict is supposed to do.

As judges of the fact, you have the right to take the evidence that you have heard from the lips of the witnesses, sift and weigh it, and you can allow as much credibility or lack of credibility as you want to everything that is said on that stand. You have the right to reject a person's testimony in toto. You have the right to accept a portion of it and reject a portion of it. You're the persons who will decide what in fact is true.

If in the course of my arguments, I refer to some law, please forgive me. That's the judge's function, and I don't mean to usurp it. If I misstate it, I'm sure he will correct me. But because they are interwoven with the facts, I may briefly allude to some principles which I will tell you about. And I will invite you to draw inferences from the facts as you find them.

Now inferences simply mean logical deductions that you make from a given set of facts. For instance, you see tracks on fresh snow. From the fact that there are tracks, you can tell whether a human being or a beast walked over the snow. If you see the footprints of a man, you know that a man has walked over the snow. You'll come to a different conclusion if an animal has walked that way.

His Honour will also tell you that if you or I were to walk into this courtroom, we would be presumed to be innocent. A defendant doesn't have to say a single blessed thing in his own defense. He can remain silent. No presumption will be engaged in against him. It would be the same if you or I were on trial for our lives. And the burden of proving beyond a reasonable doubt that the defendant is guilty of anything rests squarely with Counsel for the Commonwealth. Counsel shoulders a heavy burden. And his Honour will tell you that it's not a matter of taking all the evidence and putting it on the scales of Justice and balancing and seeing which way it tips the most. That is not the burden the prosecution is faced with. Their burden is to convince you beyond a reasonable doubt. And that means, to a moral certainty. You have to be convinced to a moral certainty. What I mean by that is, in the course of everyday life you have to evaluate and make certain decisions, certain important decisions. For instance, shall I get married, shall I have major surgery, shall I buy a house, or take a new job? These are important decisions in anyone's life. When you've taken all the evidence concerning the particular decision, you weigh it and sift it until you are convinced that you should undergo major surgery, get a new job, buy a new house. That's when you're convinced to a moral certainty. When you can make a decision of that sort and then sleep well at night, without remorse, without tossing and turning, then you're convinced beyond a reasonable doubt. And that's the burden the Commonwealth has in this case.

His Honour has told you that certain information, certain testimony in this case may only be used for limited purposes. I'll make no bones about it. But let me allude briefly to the possible verdicts in this case. You'll have four possibilities. First degree murder, second, not guilty, not guilty by reason of insanity.

Let me consider briefly the evidence that you've got before you as to a 'not guilty' possibility. Let's assume the truth as I am suggesting to you. I'm giving you the best version of the Commonwealth's case under these circumstances. Sometime prior to November 2, 1966, on four different occasions - maybe as early as February or March 1966 - the defendant supposedly made several statements to the effect that he was going to kill himself, his wife and family. Sometime around November 2, 1966, two bodies are found, wife and daughter. The fourteen year old daughter of the defendant, with terrible hatchet wounds or axe wounds about the head. Nine or so for the young girl, one or two to the wife. The defendant is seen on November 3, entering his home around 9:30 or 9:45. He's seen leaving several minutes later. That's all, that's the only testimony we have here. And several days later, November 5, he is found in the woods in Connecticut, which you've heard here ten times over, covered with excrement, vomit and so forth, and some blood stains on his clothing, on the inside or outside hem of his clothing, on his shirt-sleeves and on his tie, which are determined to be human. But we don't know whose blood, because Dr. McBey, the chemist, could not positively categorize them. He couldn't type them because of interference.

The other evidence you have as to blood was the stuff found on the man's shorts and on his handkerchief. Again, I don't recall that Dr. McBey said he could positively identify the sample as human. But that's the evidence. That's the evidence upon which the Commonwealth says we want you to be convinced beyond a reasonable doubt that Hans Schroeder murdered his wife and daughter. Indeed, you have an axe. An axe was found with blood on it. 'O' in one case, on the head of the axe. The blood of the wife was 'O', but they couldn't tell you what the blood of the daughter was.

If you find beyond a reasonable doubt on this evidence that Hans Schroeder did, in fact, kill his wife and daughter, and did it with extreme atrocity and cruelty, whatever that means, then your next question is: was he, in fact, sane at the time that he did it? That's the gut issue in this case. That's what this case has been all about from the time we sat down here two and a half weeks ago to this very instant almost.

Let's look at the evidence and see what kind of a man has been put on trial for his life in this case. Hans Schroeder, born in Germany, entered the German army when he was eighteen years of age. A few years later, he's picked up, committed to a concentration camp in Siberia for some six years. What happens there we're not quite sure of except that Dr. Mezer says he experienced a lot of horrors, saw people murdered, and whatever else we don't quite know. We do know however that he suffered minor blackouts and experienced hallucinatory activity because of, and during, that period.

Hans Schroeder is released. All his records are destroyed. He survives the camp, goes back to Germany and makes a new life for himself. He goes to work as a toymaker. Later, he becomes a bus driver. He meets Eva at some point, marries her. They have a daughter, Katarina. Sometimes later, in 1956, he comes to America and becomes an American citizen in 1961. While here, he has three more childern. He loves them all very much, and lavishes all his affection on them. He's a good family man, close to his wife and children. He works as a dishwasher when he gets here, moves on to several other jobs until he goes to work for Capital Appliance Center. Eventually, he becomes a manager of the store. Here's a fellow who can't speak English well, who has the courage to come over to a strange country after all that he has been through in Germany and Russia.

I don't know how strong he was mentally when he got out of that concentration camp. He might have been a heck of a lot stronger man when he entered it than when he got out. We don't really know for sure.

But he did have the courage and the guts to come here and start a new life.

While he is at Capital Appliance Center, a woman comes in by the name of Peggy Constanza. He never sees this woman again after she buys something there, until she is called back by the store-owner to work part-time for a two week period before Christmas, 1964. Temporary Christmas help. Hans Schroeder is working there as a manager. Peggy Constanza is there for two weeks, working with him as well as with other employees. From that time, the Schroeders and the Constanzas become friendly. Mr. and Mrs. Schroeder go out often with Mr. and Mrs. Constanza. Their childern go out together. They go out to PTA dances and Mothers' Day dances. They become very friendly. Their childern exchange visits on numerous occasions during all that time.

And there's not a whisper that anything is going on between Mrs. Constanza and Hans Schroeder. I asked Mrs. Contanza on the stand, "Did you have a happy home life?" She answered yes. "Did he have a happy home life?" She answered yes. "Was he a good family man?" Again her answer was yes. "Did you encourage that man in any way to make him think you loved him, had some affection for him?" Mrs. Constanza answered that she did not. Indeed, if in fact they were ever out together or seen together, why wasn't that evidence produced by the Commonwealth? Why wasn't Peggy Constanza's husband brought here to say, "Yes, I told him to stay away from my wife or else"?

Was there any evidence of that? Not a shred. If anything, all the information you have here is that there was nothing going on between Peggy Constanza and

Hans Schroeder. In fact, she says, "I don't think I saw him for about a year prior to November 1966," when all that happened. And when he stopped and said the things he did to her, well, she couldn't believe it. She didn't believe it, why? Because Mrs. Constanza couldn't find any reason for it.

I asked Mrs. Constanza on the stand, "Mrs. Constanza, are you sure when the first call might have been made to you when he said he was going to kill himself and his wife and family if you didn't go away with him?" She said she was not quite sure. It might have been February or March of 1966. That is, about the time that Mrs. Schroeder was having very severe problems and nervousness, and when she finally tried to commit suicide.

Peggy Constanza is not really sure about that. Not at all. The prosecution tried to get her to admit that he said to her he hated his wife. And I asked her, "Well, Mrs. Constanza, do you recall testifying here a week ago outside of the presence of the jury, when you told us about an incident where you had been stopped, first week of October, 1966, by Mr. Schroeder?" I asked her, "What did you say when you were asked whether or not he ever said he hated his wife?" And I read the transcript to her. I said, "Didn't you say at that time that he never said that, and didn't you say it again a second time when you were asked that?" Her reply was that she had said no twice. Schroeder never said that.

Mrs. Constanza received a letter from Hans Schroeder. The prosecution again tried to have her say that Hans said he hated his wife. And I had to remind her that she had testified to the Grand Jury in secret, when there were no jurors present, that all the letter said was that he was going to kill himself. Hans Schroeder had included a five dollar bill in the letter. "Put a rose on my grave for as long as the money lasts," he had written.

When I asked her what she had testified under oath back in 1968, she admitted there was not a single word said which suggested that Hans Schroeder hated his wife. I submit to you of course that it wasn't said. There's not one bit of evidence that Hans Schroeder disliked his wife.

I suppose he had the normal quarrels that we all do. That's not unusual.

Let's move on. Sometime around March of 1966, Mr. Schroeder's wife took an overdose of pills. I asked Chief Goonan whether or not, a few days later, there was also some indication of a Peeping Tom or something similar at the house. Police Chief Goonan said yes, that was the case, and that Mrs. Schroeder seemed terribly upset because of these incidents.

Did that contribute in some measure to the condition that precipitated the depression in the wife? When she, in fact, tried to commit suicide and was taken to the hospital by Mr. Schroeder himself, and where she stayed for three months, do you think that contributed to a depressed state of mind in this man? Here's a guy who comes over from Germany, doesn't understand the language very well, tries to make a go of a new life, has four children, has a job as a manager, and is working very hard to hold everything together. Suddenly his wife is in the mental hospital. He's got to come home and leave his job. He's got to take care of his four children. Did that have some effect upon this man? Was this man perhaps a good candidate for a nervous breakdown at that point?

I asked Chief Goonan on the stand if he saw Hans Schroeder often. His answer was yes, at least two or three times each week maybe, and then not for maybe another two or three weeks. And he confirmed that he found Schroeder depressed during this time. Is that an indication that he was down in the dumps or at least a good candidate for it at that time?

Let's not assume at this time whether or not Hans Schroeder had some kind of infatuation for the woman Peggy Constanza. She disavows any involvement. The truth is, there is no evidence to suggest an infatuation.

I submit to you that Hans Schroeder arrived at a point in his life where he could not deal with it any longer. His prior background left him in such a state that he slid into the very depths of depression. This has been testified to on numerous occasions. And during the first week of 1966 he said to Peggy Constanza that he would kill himself, his wife, and family if she didn't run away with him. And she told him he was crazy, or words to that effect. She couldn't believe it. She was shocked. He repeated it again a week later. Was that a sort of traumatic event that might trigger a mental illness in this man, given his background? Was it? Why wouldn't it be?

We spend billions of dollars to put a man up in space. Before we put him up we don't know what effect putting him up in space, being alone, will have on his mind. That's because we know so little about the mind. But before Allan Shepherd went up we spent billions in tests to find out. It's something we don't say anything about. And yet, when a Vietnam vet, a P.O.W., is released after several years in prison, he comes home a free man and commits suicide a short time later. Why? He's been released. He's free. What effect did that incarceration have upon him? Do we know what effect six years in the Siberian concentration camp had on Hans Schroeder? Was he susceptible? Was he as vulnerable as the Vietnam vet who was released, came home, and committed suicide a short time ago?

Ladies and gentlemen, when you go out to deliberate, the judge doesn't say, "Okay, Jurors, when you get out in the Jury Room leave your common sense behind and make a decision." You have a right to take that good, God-given common sense that you were born with, to use your experience as men and women of affairs and apply that to what you see and hear in this courtroom. Was Hans Schroeder a candidate for a breakdown sometime? If Dr. Woodward says you can get this particular psychotic depressive reaction by a cut on the hand, by having a child go off to school, is that any less traumatic than a man who either fantasizes or has something going with a woman and is rejected? Is that any less traumatic, given the totality of this man's background? If a cut on the hand is going to do it, why wouldn't this rejection?

Whether or not we moralize about his involvement or non-involvement, the question we must ask ourselves is whether it did precipitate something, a mental illness of such proportions that it caused him to do something that is just inconceivable. Totally inconceivable.

Sometime around November 2, 1966, Hans Schroeder returned to his home. The Commonwealth will make a great to-do about the fact that he was going to get a raise, whatever the raise was going to be. It might be a two dollar raise, we don't know. It would have been nice to know what kind of a raise he was going to get, to see how happy one was likely to be. Maybe it was a two dollar raise. The Commonwealth will make a great to-do about the fact that he was going to get a car with a two-way radio to help him with his sales calls. Was that sufficient to make this man well again? And supposedly he was going to be telling his wife about this news. Here's a man who supposedly doesn't like his wife, but is supposedly going to tell his wife about his new two-way radio. Does that show he has some concern, some feeling, for her? He still loves her at the time. Could it be so, even though he might be just a bit mentally deficient?

He returns home and he's had a few drinks. He has no record of alcoholism in his past history. Nothing, and Dr. Mezer confirms this. If there was any alcohol in his record, wouldn't you think the Commonwealth would've produced it for you and said, "Look, here, he's an alcoholic. One or two drinks, why, he goes wacky." But the truth is Hans Schroeder is anything but alcoholic. He's a respectable kind of guy. He was head of a bowling league, vice president of the P.T.A. in his town. An upright, upstanding kind of guy. Police Chief Goonan says that. Sergeant Darsch says that. Mrs. Constanza says that. In fact, the Commonwealth's own witnesses say that.

Maybe he was an alcoholic. This is a tongue in cheek kind of argument. There is no evidence whatsoever that the man drank excessively. But the

Commonwealth could well say to you, "Why not, why wasn't the event or events just a product of a drunken stupor?" But if the man was drunk when he got home, why does his wife offer him an anisette? Is she going to give that to a husband who she thinks is drunk? Was he just upset to his stomach with an ulcerous condition that he'd had for some time? I submit to you that this man was not drunk at that time. I submit to you that he was mentally ill for a period of time.

As Dr. Woodward says, which comes on over a period of weeks and months. Then it must've been there for some period of time, it's something because the mental hospital, Bridgewater State Hospital, diagnosed him on November 7 as being a psychotic depressive. And if Dr. Woodward's testimony is to be believed at all, then that particular state of mind, that mental disease, was there for some weeks prior.

And now Hans Schroeder goes to bed. We don't know what happened except from Hans Schroeder's own words that he gave to Dr. Mezer and gave to the hospital. And he said he awoke to a buzzer, found himself kneeling by his son's bed, found his wife and daughter dead, took his children out. The rest is testimony from others who saw him supposedly in a motel and then again in the woods.

Why is it so inconsistent that he has no memory of what happened? Dr. Mezer says a lack of memory and confusion is consistent with a psychotic depressive reaction. What is inconsistent about that? The Commonwealth says he remembered everything else, and that his lack of memory of specific details is simply a matter of convenience.

Certainly, when you look at the excerpts from the hospital report, which you will have before you, you will find things that don't always benefit him. And some that do. Is that convenience? And I suppose the Commonwealth is going to say, "Look how normal he looked when he was at that motel." Why, Mr. Pettit said he looked normal, he asked directions to Cape Cod. But he had just come from Cape Cod. Did he have to ask directions back? Mr. Pettit also said he looked tired. Tired from what? Well, from his driving, he said. Perhaps from something else you don't know anything about, Mr. Pettit. I submit that this tiredness was tiredness of the mind that this man had been suffering from for a long time.

When the man is found in the woods on the fifth, I suppose we can say he faked. He faked it. He's out there, incontinent of urine and faeces, vomit all over himself. He had taken a lot of pills, three hundred aspirin tablets. We know there was aspirin found in his blood. Faked it all. Or maybe he was trying in some way to do away with himself. Maybe he was less than totally normal. Maybe he was mentally ill at that time and was trying to kill himself.

When he came out of the woods and said to the hunters, "Shoot me, shoot me, shoot me," he said it several times. Charles Sanga said that. Do you suppose he wanted to be killed at that time? The Commonwealth will say, "Well, he was so guilt-stricken, so stricken in conscience, that he wanted to kill himself and be killed." He had expressed a desire to kill himself numerous times prior to that time. And then again on that day. Isn't it equally consistent with the facts that this man was mentally deranged, mentally upset at the time? Dr. Mezer said it's very consistent with the fact that a person can be psychotic and still do the normal things. It happens in hospitals every day. People get up, bathe, clean themselves, clothe themselves. They can go through periods when the illness is not as severe as at other times. It goes up like a thermometer. Remember I asked Dr. Woodward that, "Doctor, isn't it like 103, 104, and then back again?" Disease has various gradations. I submit that is in fact the case.

And you have been given the benefit here of psychiatric testimony. You were given the benefit of a psychiatrist who is now dead, and another psychiatrist who just did not happen to see Hans Schroeder. You weren't given the benefit of a Dr. Samuel Allen who saw this man when he was the Acting Medical Director. It doesn't hold water to say that the defendant could have called him as well. Or did you think that Dr. Sam Allen might have said something which would contradict what other psychiatrists have said?

Dr. Woodward says this man was not psychotically depressed. That he was not a psychotic depressive any time either before or after. But we know that the hospital report says, yes, he was a psychotic depressive on November seventh at least, and maybe for sometime before that. Now, that's not consistent, is it, if the Commonwealth produces a doctor who saw him and says he was a psychotic depressive on the seventh of November, and Dr. Woodward now has to explain how it can be so if this particular mental disease occurs over several weeks. Because that would take it back over November second, doesn't it? Then how would he get around that inconsistency? I can't cross-examine Dr. Allen in that respect, and that weakens our case.

Dr. Woodward comes in here. He says, yes, psychiatry is an imprecise science and difficult. It is difficult, is it not, to determine what's in a person's mind at any given time, even if you could look at him a week or two later? How difficult is it when you don't even see the guy and you're asked to come in to evaluate the man?

Dr. Woodward wasn't brought in to treat Mr. Schroeder. He wasn't a treatment doctor. He was a testimony doctor. The Commonwealth put him on to testify as to the man's sanity. Based on what? On exhibit Z, excerpts from the hospital report. And I asked Dr. Woodward, "Doctor, haven't you seen about ninety eight percent of your patients, and isn't it important that a psychiatrist sees his patients before he diagnoses the illness?" And he replied, of course, it was important.

Of course it is. Do you accept with as much credibility the testimony of a man who has never seen the other person? If you called a psychiatrist and said, "Doctor, I've got a problem," and he said, "Tell me what it is and I'll tell you what your diagnosis is, and I'll send you the bill." Would you go visit such a doctor?

Dr. Woodward testified strictly on the basis of that particular exhibit, nothing more. I asked him in one question after the other, "Did you consider this? Did you consider that?" For instance, had he considered Schroeder's incarceration in a concentration camp. He said, "I've considered it, but I rejected it." Why? From what I've read I know what Russian prison camps might be like. They're not nice places like Walpole.

And I said, "Doctor, would it be important to know something of what this man suffered at that time as an important piece of history?" He replied, "No, it wouldn't be important."

If you, ladies and gentlemen of the Jury, were psychiatrists, do you think it would be important to go into something you'd call the man's background before you evaluated him? Would it be important information that you'd like to know? I think Dr. Woodward was straining to prove the man sane. If he had said, "Yes, I think it's important, Mr. Piscitelli," I believe I would've had more respect for his opinions. But he did not. "No, it's not important," he said.

Of course it is important to know all the history you can about a man, especially a man given to hallucinations. I asked him that: "Doctor, did you consider the fact that this man hallucinated during that period?" Yes, but he discounted that. "And did you consider the fact that he had minor blackouts during that period?" Yes, but he'd discounted that. "And did you consider, Doctor, the fact that the man's wife tried to commit suicide and that he had to leave work and take care of four children and that he was depressed and seemed to be depressed during that period for several months prior to November 2, 1966?". "Yes," he replied, "I did, but I discounted that." Again I asked, "Did you consider that a Dr. Briggs said he was agitated two or three days before November 2, 1966? Agitated and upset." Yes, he did, but he had discounted that too. Gave it no weight whatsoever.

What did Dr. Woodward consider? Just that very narrow portion the government gave him, what they wanted to pick and choose to have him decide on. How much did he eliminate or neglect to talk about? How much weight, then, are we to put on that man's opinions?

And I said, "Well, Dr. Woodward, do you consider it important to be able to see the man? Would you have considered it important to have been able to see him on November 5, 1966, to examine him and talk to him?" And what did he say? He said, "No."

Do you believe that to be so? If you were a doctor at that time, wouldn't you want to have seen this man? Of course you would. Do you suppose Dr. Woodward was, again, straining to justify his opinion. I submit to you that he was. If he had been straightforward, he'd have said, "You bet. If I had seen him it would've helped me in my diagnosis." Of course, it would have. I think it's obvious. You've got to apply your common sense.

The Commonwealth then brought forward a transcript of a Dr. Lawrence Barrows. His Honour will instruct you that, if a person dies and his testimony is given in a court of law, and there's been a chance to cross-examine him down below, then his testimony can go in, subject to certain objections.

Did you hear Dr. Barrows' background when it was read to you by the Commonwealth? He said he had his last four years in psychiatry, two of them at Bridgewater. Prior to that, he spent about twenty years, if I recall correctly, as a pathologist or a neurologist or something like that. He supervised psychiatric residents. Never once did he mention in his testimony that he was a psychiatrist.

And what about his background compared to Dr. Mezer's? Did he publish books, teach, or attend some of these top-notch schools like Harvard and Tufts? Was he at any time qualified as an expert? No. I submit that he wasn't an expert.

Dr. Barrows was asked to determine when this man became a psychotic depressive. He said on the seventh, basing his opinion on a chance conversation with Dr. Briggs, a general practitioner, who had treated Hans Schroeder's children a few days before. Dr. Briggs had observed that Hans Schroeder was upset and agitated but not abnormally so. And that was the basis, the whole basis, I think the words were 'the principal basis', of Dr. Barrows' opinion that Hans Schroeder was, in fact, sane.

I want to ask you, if a man appears to be agitated and upset two days before a terrible, terrible killing, if in fact he did it, wouldn't that be some indication that something is going on in the man's mind? This doctor was a general practitioner. He wasn't a psychiatrist. For him to say 'not abnormally so', what does that mean? Something was going on in that man's mind to cause him to be upset and agitated. Dr. Barrows attributes it to financial worries and the fact that Mrs. Schroeder was rather sick at the time. How much stock do you place in that opinion?

On the other hand, you had Dr. Mezer. Here's a person who has written a textbook in psychiatry, who teaches it at the top schools, in law schools as a matter of fact, and at hospitals. Such a man, is he going to prostitute himself to say something he doesn't firmly believe in? You'll remember I asked him tough questions on the stand. I asked, "Doctor, how do you know this guy wasn't lying to you?" He said he had some objective signs to go by. "How do you know he wasn't conning you?" Dr. Mezer said he believed the man.

Dr. Mezer gave you his considered opinion that, on November 2, 1966, Hans Schroeder was unable to appreciate the criminality or the wrongfulness of any conduct he engaged in. He gave his opinion couched in the definition of insanity in this Commonwealth, that the man could not conform his conduct to normality because of a mental disease. Is the doctor going to say something that can't be supported by the record?

Here's a man who has seen Hans Schroeder. Not like Dr. Woodward who comes in seven years late. Dr. Mezer saw him on November 11 for the first time, as I recall. He saw him again on the twenty fifth, and on many other occasions thereafter. The man's past history played a major role as a firm basis for his opinions. How did Dr. Mezer come across to you? Again, it is you who have the right to attach as much credibility or lack of credibility as you want to a witness.

I asked Dr. Mezer whether or not any statements this man made following November 2, 1966, were the products of a rational mind. He said, "No, they were not." He said that the psychotic depressive reaction he diagnosed was a major mental illness. And, most importantly, he said it was highly suspect whether the man committed the killings or not. Consider the condition the man was in. Didn't every sign indicate that the man was suffering from something at the time? A mental illness, perhaps? I asked the doctor whether or not the manner of the killings had any effect upon his opinion that a person who is said to have loved his daughter as much as he did could have done it in a sane condition, even assuming it was his hand that lifted the axe nine times. "Yes it does," he said. It was not the act of a sane man at the time. It's something you'd find impossible to believe of a sane person. When I asked Chief Goonan about his thoughts when he first heard of Hans Schroeder's involvement, whether he found it hard it believe, I think his answer summed it up nicely. "Yes, I did," he said. "I found it impossible to believe."

Was there anywhere in this case an attempt to hide an axe? Hide bodies? The Commonwealth wants to make this man out as a terrible killer, as a man who knew precisely what he was doing. But the axe was in plain view. Does that sound like the product of a rational mind, or of a man who is mentally incompetent at the time, has no recollection of what he has done, and leaves everything out in the open, assuming again that he's the one who did it? Isn't that a fact in this case that is more consistent with a person who was deranged at the time?

The Commonwealth wants you to believe what this man did was a rational, lucid act. I submit to you that you don't need psychiatrists to tell you whether a man is insane or not. Get rid of all psychiatrists here. Take them and forget that they ever testified. Do you need somebody to tell you that a man with his background, with his history, was not in fact insane when this happened? The evidence cries out that is, in fact, the case.

My job is about done. I have tried to convey to you a picture of this man. A good, hard-working man who fits the picture that Dr. Woodward would have you believe, a good conscientious man who is a fit subject to become a psychotic depressive. I have tried to convey as best as I can to you the feelings that might have been in this man's mind on November second, nineteen sixty six. And I'd be lying to you if I told you that I won't be happy when I sit down in a few minutes. I will be pleased because this has been a burden on my shoulders now for months and months. Now I have taken it off my shoulders and transferred it to yours. In a very short time, if not today then tomorrow morning, suddenly you'll have the very awesome responsibility, perhaps the most awesome responsibility you have ever had in your lives, because you will have in your hands the power of life or death over another human being. What you say when you return your verdict will determine this man's future.

You know he has been incarcerated in Massachusetts now for six years up to the present time. You know that for some twelve years of this man's life, he has been in some prison or the other. You know that if he believes he did it that is going to carry with him the rest of his life. He's got to live with it. Whatever torment that brings with it will be a part of him. No amount of punishment which you can impose on him is going to be any greater than that punishment and torment this man has suffered, is suffering, thinking that he killed the one thing in his life that he loved so greatly, his family. The one thing for whose freedom and opportunities he left his fatherland. Surely, he will carry something terrible to his grave. You won't make him suffer any more than he has been suffering.

If in the course of this trial I have said something which has offended you, please forgive me. Chalk up your displeasure against me, and not my client. Please assume it to be the zeal of a lawyer who sincerely believes that his client was in fact not guilty by reason of insanity at the time certain crimes were allegedly committed. Please tell me sometime how terrible I was, if you will, but hold it against me and not my client.

I have a great deal of faith in the jury system. I firmly believe that twelve people like you, when you apply your collective common sense, must necessarily come up with the true verdict. And I have the utmost faith that, when you look at the picture in its totality, you will find that Hans Schroeder was in fact unable to conform his conduct to the requirements of law.

And when the Commonwealth says that he laid the axe the first time at the head of his daughter, was he sane at that time? This gentle, peaceful man that Chief Goonan describes him to be? And when he laid the second blow, if he did, to the head of his daughter whom he loved so much, was he really sane? And when the third blow was again laid to the head of that girl, was he sane then, this man who, witnesses have testified, always had great tenderness, compassion and affection for his family? And when he laid the fourth, fifth, sixth, seventh, eighth, and ninth blows. Was he sane then, if in fact he did it, this man who has said that Katarina was his favourite?

Ladies and gentlemen of the jury, thank you for your patience. Thank you for your courtesy throughout the course of this trial. I respectfully suggest to you that, when you've sifted all of the evidence together, you'll come to one conclusion. That conclusion, in Chief Goonan's words when he heard of Schroeder's involvement: "I couldn't believe it. I couldn't believe it." And I ask you to find the same, that you can't believe it. This man was not in fact sane at the time this happened.

11

Lies, Lies, Lies, I lie awake all night and think of the lies all day. In my dreams, even my daydreams, I can hardly recognize them for lies. I was not going to let it happen to me all over again, even though, as far as I could see, it was all over for me. I couldn't imagine the jury falling for Piscitelli's line. I began to perspire at the thought of returning to Walpole for good. I still couldn't believe I mightn't have to return to Walpole. That possibility hardly crossed my mind. At the thought of the jury's verdict echoing through the courtroom, I was seized with a violent, choking sensation. It seemed something was trying to squeeze the life out of me. I never thought I would come out of it alive. Earlier, when they led me back to the adjoining cell, I was sorry to miss the pleasant, lazy sunlight I had seen trying to break through the massive courtroom windows. The familiar sight of the dark bars surrounding me was stifling. They seemed to have followed me most of my life. Was it because I have always been poor, in a manner of speaking that is? After all, I wouldn't have been able to afford a lawyer. It was good and kind of Piscitelli to take me on. And then it occurred to me that my condition had nothing to do with what little I had earned, with what little I had saved. But wait. If the vicious negroes I had encountered in Walpole were part of the scum, I too was scum, floating in the same cesspool as them, chained to the same garbage can as them.

This was the lie I had walked into like a fool. I had sold myself. For what? I wish I could crawl back to Germany. I wish I could bring back the music I once loved. Once it followed me everywhere, in war, before and even after the war. The music rang in my head as we rolled through villages and towns, the houses deserted, the streets empty. We would pass women and children, sometimes standing alone, sometimes in silent clusters, their faces full of amazement and fear. A few moments in front of my eyes, then they were memory.

I remember our column stopping one day at the crest of a gentle valley. Suddenly, it was quieter than I ever seemed to remember. At such halts, it would be hours before the head rid itself of the constant whir of engines and the sound of clanking metal. On that day, at the edge of the valley, a gentle breeze blew through the leaves filling me with a strange elation. I leapt out of the turret, washed my face, and sat alone on a grassy knoll. And all the time I kept hearing the music of the gods entering Valhalla.

You know, if I never took Eva to the Opera House in Wiesbaden I doubt it was because we were poor. I was probably just as poor before I left for the war. I think it was because I had lost God. More than the loss of God, I think I had forgotten Wagner. It fills me with sadness and regret to think I avoided the place I loved so much. I remember walking past the place though, hand in hand with Eva, and talking about how nice, how grand, it would be to go to the opera once. Instead, here I was in a back room of the courthouse.

It was a small area within which they were holding me, barely nine feet by nine. It seemed too small to allow me even to move my head, and it was shrinking every minute. I would never let myself get behind bars again. I heard voices telling me I'd get used to it, that it was nothing. I had heard such voices in Siberia too. I had also known those who, after years surrounded by barbed wire, could seal their memories behind an impassable wall between the past and present.

I had tried to follow such men into a state of forgetfulness and hopelessness. But my defences were never too strong. When they gave way, the memories crashed through the breach, seizing my mind with redoubled fury. No, I didn't wish to return to Walpole, to be asked, "Know anyone out here? Someone who can protect you." Or, "How much money do you have?" I had none. I was part of the trash.

It is hard to imagine that I have never been too far away from my first glimpse of the prison's high, whitewashed walls set back among the trees. It will remain engraved in my memory. The drive past the parking area, the steps leading to the white stucco building known as Outer Central, the long rooms with walls piled high with plaster lamps, toys, wooden furniture, and leather handbags made by prisoners, none of these held even the remotest suggestion of what awaited me inside. It was only after the electronically-controlled steel door had slammed behind me in the personnel trap, and I looked up to see an officer peering down at me through a glass plate in the floor of a room above the trap, that I began to feel my blood running cold.

The limits to my freedom, in the land of the free, were clearly marked. True, there was a great deal of freedom inside the prison. One could visit other inmates in their cells or, with a pass from the block guard, even visit those in other sections. But the truth was that one's freedom didn't extend over one's own body. In that respect, it was no different from Yercevo.

Prison didn't seem any rougher than the world outside. To survive, one had to learn how to out-fox, out-manoeuvre, out-think, out-slick the other guy. Or you lost. This was the simple rule inside the prison. I found it no different from the outside where I had lost too. My greatest sense of loss was probably the loss of my fatherland, the loss of Germany. I had become part of the excrement of war. They had pulled down a proud people into a pit of excrement and I had nodded my acceptance, smiled, and shaken hands with an enemy which had auctioned off our manhood.

I quickly learnt the wisdom of remaining on friendly terms with a couple of inmate big shots. I was convinced that, under certain circumstances, their good will could save my life. But there were other situations where no one could've helped me. That's when I tried to back down as gracefully as possible. I would swallow my pride, tuck my tail between my legs, and run like hell.

Yes, that's what I had been reduced to. Strangely enough, I felt no shame, no remorse over my state. It seemed to be the special prerogative of power. Do unto others lest the others do it to you. I have read, heard about the terrible things the Germans did to others. Did I take part in any of it? Certainly not. Do I accept responsibility for any of it? I most certainly do. And why not? Ours was the noblest brotherhood of all. But, for the deaths of my wife and daughter, I will not accept any responsibility. I loved them. I could never have done to them what they showed me. Never, Never, Never.

Yet, there were many in prison who believed I deserved harsher punishment than what I had received. One could get killed for that. I found it was very easy to die for simple, unimportant reasons. There was always something one had that another inmate wanted. It could be a radio, a TV set, drugs, money, a girl to sneak in pills, one's body if one was young, one's friendship if one was big and strong. Harry was sympathetic throughout. "You did what you had to do," he said, "They're scum, anyway." This, after I had told him about Joey, whose parentage I didn't know of, nor cared to know. To think of him in bed with Katarina was more of an insult than I was prepared to suffer. Oh Katarina! I keep asking myself over and over, why did you break my heart? Why did you add to my torment?

The National Prisoners Reform Association started at Walpole in late spring of 1972. It was a bizarre election from the beginning to the end, with threats and stuffed ballots at every turn. The president took his orders straight from the Mafia, I was told. He was serving a life sentence for the murder of a Boston detective who caught him in a robbery. A vice-president was serving a three hundred year sentence, after he and two friends came across a young couple in a lovers' lane. While the two friends mercilessly beat up the man, our vice president was busy pushing a tree branch up between the girl's legs. Then they tossed the young couple in the car, set it afire, and drove off. The young girl somehow crawled out of the car and managed to attract help. Now she was spending her life in a nut-house. I had to scrape and bow before such men as I had once done in front of Klevshin.

With such inmates, it was difficult to imagine the prison being run by the superintendent. The inmate leaders in Cellblock Two were the real bosses. It was they who ran the prostitution ring. To carry on their business, the association leaders had taken over the prison hospital. Whenever Harry wanted to enjoy sexual favours, he would have to approach a 'High Command' member. The High Command collected the money, informed its contact on the street, and arranged for a girl to visit the inmate on a specified day.

Harry was breathing hard in anticipation all day one Thursday. In the afternoon, he went to the hospital complaining of severe chest pains and swore to the doctor he was about to die. Why take any chances? The doctor readily admitted him. When Sue arrived the following day to visit Harry, she was promptly ushered into the hospital ward. She was locked in the hospital cell with Harry. The guard returned at the end of visiting hour to let Sue out. Harry improved dramatically after that, poorer by twenty dollars but rich in memories until the next time.

I had no money in my prison bank account. Harry had plenty. He would ask for transfers from time to time, which were almost like cheques. I know he'd buy Valium and Purple Haze LSD whenever he felt desperate, but where he found so much money was a mystery to me. I doubt he had any visitors who would slip him a twenty dollar bill in the belief he would use it to buy food and cigarettes. That was what one paid for five pills, twenty dollars.

Harry got into trouble over Talwin, a pain-killer prisoners diluted with water and shot into the veins to get a quick high. On three separate occasions, Harry was beaten up and sent to the hospital. Each time, he was prescribed Talwin to deaden the pain of his injuries. He never got to swallow any more than the first pills. As soon as he came back to the block, he was relieved of his prescription. "If we find any Talwin on you," he was told, 'you'll get your fuckin' head beaten in again." As a favour, they gave Harry a few shots of scotch whenever the stuff could be smuggled in from outside as cans of apple juice duly marked with supermarket labels. I was an occasional beneficiary too.

A fellow prisoner named Gonzalves refused to cooperate over Talwin. A few of the guys collected some lacquer from the paint shop, and torched his cell. Gonzalves died swiftly in one roaring whoosh. My friend, Albert de Salvo was killed on November 26. I liked him, even though many of the inmates were jealous of Al's wealth. Everyone believed he had a couple of giant bank accounts from the proceeds of his book and movie rights. He also ran a profitable jewelry business selling pins and bracelets in the prison's outer lobby and through various merchants scattered throughout Massachusetts. A card went with every piece of jewelry: Handmade by Albert de Salvo. The thugs were constantly shaking Al down for money. I never heard him complain.

With Harry as a friend, Walpole lost all its fears for me. The rules were tough, but soon as you learnt to roll with the punches, you learnt to survive. Still, I must confess it was possible to tire of such survival, especially since each new day seemed no different than the previous days. Our passions and perversions soon became an accepted part of our selves.

One learnt to turn away from things that seemed human, for things human were incomprehensible to most of us. If human contact — the kind most of us crave — seemed rare in the world outside, it was virtually non-existent within the prison walls. Harry, of course, was an exception. That's why I found it so difficult to understand Harry. One thing a criminal can easily understand is another criminal. But Harry was no criminal. I could never share with him that irrationality, a common infection of blind madness and defiance, that tied the rest of us in bonds of hostility. The law had branded us, herded us within these walls, and locked our destinies in the sewer. Now we could all feed on one another, all except Harry. The most accessible like me were also the most vulnerable. That's why I needed Harry.

I once overheard a warden telling a particularly vicious neighbour, "Look, settle down and get yourself a kid." And the guy went hunting in earnest, ignoring those he knew to be gays. He finally settled for a young college kid who didn't want anything to do with him. A week later, the prison officials found the kid in a pool of blood, his face bashed in, and knife gashes on his legs. I asked Harry why the kid remained silent, why his assailant went merrily about his business. And Harry asked me if the kid would dare tell the officials, "Yeah, Mike was trying to fuck me."

Harry is the only person I got. He's warm, he's alive, he's a human being. He's someone I can stand next to, in prison as in war. It was all the same. I stuck to Harry because there was no one else. Just this other person to reach out to, to touch, to put my arms around him. Everything else was forbidden. I needed Harry to feel like we were both in the same pot, sinking together, coming alive together. Everything else was unreal. Some prisoners had forgotten what it was to fuck a woman. Others kept promising their women they'd do anything for them once they got out. Like lick her pussy every night. Harry warned me that the knives were real, the knives they put on young boys. So was the hatred and the desperation. Harry asked me if I had ever heard anyone say, "I'm getting out of here and I'm gonna find myself a decent job." I hadn't. But I had heard plenty saying how they planned to screw every moment of their freedom, young and supple broads. And I had heard plenty who couldn't wait to shoot themselves full of heroin.

Surely, all such thoughts are meaningless to me. I am destined to rot in Walpole. This time they will put me inside and throw the key away. I know that's what they're going to do.

My heart aches for Katarina. You were so innocent, so sweet, so pure. Why did you have to get mixed up with Joey? I might have forgiven her, but Eva was so adamant. I never liked Joey myself. There was something ingratiating about him I took an instant dislike to. Late one night I was awakened by Eva shouting from the family room below. I was fast asleep and had no idea when Eva had left the bed. Startled, I jumped up and rushed downstairs. I was appalled to see Joey and Katarina side by side on the sofa, clinging to a comforter drawn up to their necks. Their faces were white with fear, while Eva's was flushed with anger. My own rage and sense of shame subsided somewhat at the sight of the half-naked Joey being shoved out of the front door by an incensed Eva. Looking totally bewildered and fearful, Joey stumbled down the steps, clutching his shoes and clothes in a crumpled mass. The darkness swallowed him up and he never came to the house again. I never heard Katarina mention his name one more time.

Eva made up her mind Katarina had to be punished. "But I love him," she pleaded. Eva slapped her soundly across her face. A fiery red streak flashed over her cheek, only to be overshadowed by the even deeper red of the blood that gushed out of her nose. I could not help myself as I instinctively held out my hand and found Katarina in my arms, her warm blood spreading over my shirt a stain that would never wash away. It was probably at that moment I realized that whatever love I had for Eva had withered away. Some of the anger that filled my heart spilled over and began to poison my love for Katarina as well. Even as I held her in my arms I realized we were drifting apart. The realization broke my heart. I could find no reason for my other children. I had no idea why Eva had ever borne the boys or little Carolyn for that matter. They were good kids, but they belonged to a world I was a stranger to. I couldn't see them as having anything in common with me.

I feel strangely detached from my sons. I have no feeling for them any more. That is not to say I don't wish them well. I hope they can still see the baseball games like the ones we enjoyed in town and, on rare occasions, in Fenway Park. I wish them well wherever they are in northern New York State.

Sometimes I wish we had never set foot on this land. It takes too much effort, too much pain, to re-live

Wiesbaden in Brockton. One can only live it in one's dreams. But life is easy — or so it seems to me — if one can invest in other dreams. Eva managed the change so well. She erased the grandeur of Wiesbaden from her memory and replaced it with — with what? And I didn't even try to stop her.

Come to think of it, I too must've worshipped the same God as her, or we would've surely quarrelled. As I look back over what I've lived for I can't see any reason. As I imagine what there is to live for, I can't see anything either. Yes, I hear many voices inside my head. They all sound like the voice of reason. Can it be true? Each voice overturns the other. Each time reason triumphs?

Even the most trying of my days brightened up when I came home in the evening if only I could hear Katarina practising her piano. It was a breath of fresh, fragrant air in an otherwise musty day. She would stop in the middle of her Mozart or whoever and look to me for that approving smile, a kiss, or simply my special feeling of pleasure which I could never hide.

Gradually, our lives took on a kind of mechanical quality, of unrelieved tedium. We were much better off than we ever were in Wiesbaden, but it seemed the real laughter — the loud, uninhibited kind — had gone out of our lives. I spent very little time with Carolyn or Dennis or Chris. It was not that I didn't love them or couldn't find time for them. They were lovable, good-looking kids. But it was impossible for them to displace Katarina from the centre of my affections. And there was nothing outside of the centre.

There was also something that kept me from giving my love entirely and unquestioningly to Katarina, and

I often railed against myself for this. Harry had sown the seeds of suspicion in my heart. They stuck there. I found no means of cleaning them out of my mind. I would catch myself raging over Eva fraternizing with the Americans in Wiesbaden. Oh yes! did she not seem unusually eager to come to America. Besides, wasn't there something sneaky, something obscene, about her relationship with Hans Wiegel? There were days when my suspicions held my heart in a vice of steel. If then I felt indifferently towards Katarina, I think my feelings for Eva bordered on the hostile.

And what about Peggy? Did she or did she not come into my life? Was Timmy a dream too? I wept for Timmy. I persisted with Peggy for four long years that now seem like a lifetime. She had told me things I dare not repeat to anyone. It would only cause her more hurt. I guess she sort of circled around it and decided to leave it alone.

"Look at yourself," Eva said to me. "You're a smaller man than I knew in Wiesbaden. Prove yourself. Do something about Katarina."

Katarina was my heart and soul. It was for her that we set out to conquer the new world. Or so it seemed to me once. Now I had lost her too. "Speak to her," Eva hissed at me. "She'll fill up with baby and bring shame upon us all."

12

At the very beginning of this case I made an opening statement outlining for you what it is the Commonwealth intended to prove. You may recall I told you that about a year prior to the event, the defendant told a woman that he loved her, that if she didn't run away with him he'd kill himself and his family. Several times during that year, he made essentially the same statement to that woman. In early October, 1966, he forced the woman off the road in her automobile, walked over to her and said, "I love you. If you don't run away with me I'll kill myself and I'll kill my family." And, finally, about a week prior to the horrible event in this case, he called up the woman and said the same thing.

I've introduced further evidence that on November 3, the defendant was in his home. He is home on the morning of that day, according to neighbours. On the fourth day of November, the defendant made some telephone calls and said words to the effect, "I've done something terrible, and my wife and child are dead. They're D-E-A-D. Call the police." Several people have testified to these phone conversations.

Some policemen have testified that when Hans Schroeder was found and asked, "Are you Hans Schroeder, wanted for the murder of wife and daughter?" he replied, "I'm Hans Schroeder, the murderer. I did it. I did it." Later on that day, he is quoted as saying, "How can you be so nice to me after what I've done? Why don't you shoot me?"

Then I told you we'd introduce evidence to show that the defendant, Hans Schroeder, was legally sane at the time of the event on November 2 or November 3, 1966.

Well, ladies and gentlemen of the jury, I submit to you that I have introduced proof on all of those points. And, except for the question of sanity, on which I'll speak later, all of that evidence, all of that testimony, was totally and completely uncontradicted.

So we don't have here, as in so many criminal cases, the classic issue of credibility. That is to say, as between two conflicting stories, who are we to believe? Here, we have testimony from several witnesses which remains totally and completely uncontradicted.

I expect his Honour will instruct you as to the various kinds of proof in a case, the direct proof and the circumstantial evidence proof. In this case, obviously we don't have any direct proof. There was no one there who saw Hans Schroeder perform these acts except the defendant himself. There is no other witness that we can produce, no one who'll say, "Ah-hah! Yes, I did see him do that."

I'm afraid we have to rely on circumstantial evidence in this case. And just as the defense gave you the illustration of the footprints in the snow, so I too must ask you to infer that Hans Schroeder did, indeed, perform these acts, that Hans Schroeder did indeed kill his wife and daughter on the day in question.

I argue before you, ladies and gentlemen, that he did because he said that he would. He told a woman several times during the year, "I'm going to kill my wife and daughter." He said other things as well. That he was going to kill himself, going to kill his whole family. Specifically, he said words to the effect, "I'm going to kill my wife and daughter if you don't run away with me."

Hans Schroeder lived in his home with his family. No one else lived there. He was found with blood on his clothes, and we know from the chemist that it was human blood found on his tie, his shirt, his coat and pants. There was blood, we're unsure whether it was human or not, on his underwear. That blood couldn't be typed because of chemical interference, chemical change. But there's no question in this case that there was human blood on Hans Schroeder's clothes at the time he was apprehended by the State Police.

Perhaps I shouldn't belabour this, after the defense has said that insanity is the gut issue in this case. but I argue to you that Hans Schroeder killed his wife, killed his daughter, because he said he would in no uncertain terms. He said he would, and no one else had the opportunity to do it. It was done in his own home. It was done at a time when he was there, inside his home. Ladies and gentlemen of the jury, I argue to you that no one else in the world could possibly, possibly, have killed these women except the defendant in this case. He said he would, and he had nearly the exclusive opportunity to do so.

But, as you've been told, the gut issue is insanity. When Hans Schroeder did this did he have the substantial capacity to appreciate the criminality of his conduct? Did he have the substantial capacity to conform his conduct to the requirements of law? Well, ladies and gentlemen, we have a statement by Hans Schroeder on the fourth of November wherein he says over the telephone, "I've just done something terrible. My wife and child are dead."

Does that sound like someone who just couldn't appreciate the criminality of his conduct? Or does it sound like someone who knew very well that he had committed a crime, that he had done a heinous deed? He said that he had done something terrible. Doesn't that show appreciation, knowledge, that he had done a criminal act?

Again, on that same day, he calls someone else and says the same thing, "I've killed my wife." Does that sound like an amnesiac, someone who can't remember anything at all, as he would have Dr. Mezer believe? Later on, on the fifth of November, he says to a State policeman, "I did it, I did it, I did it. I'm Hans Schroeder, the murderer." Does that sound like someone who didn't appreciate the criminality of his conduct?

I could go on and on. From Chief Goonan's testimony: "How can you be so nice to me after what I've done?" We have here a clear appreciation of the criminality of a deed. Here's a man we're supposed to believe, according to the defendant's case, that he was legally insane. And yet, he goes down and checks into a motel with his children. He asks directions about restaurants and so forth. The manager of the motel saw nothing unremarkable about his behavior. He found him clean-shaven, correct, neatly dressed.

Is there something about the manager of a motel, something special about that kind of a job, which would induce a person to look very closely at anyone registering at the motel? I submit there is. Here's a man whose livelihood depends upon having guests in the motel who aren't going to rip off the place, who aren't going to have drunken parties. He's looking for someone who looks like Solid Harry, certainly, a guy who just appears like an average American citizen, doesn't appear, certainly doesn't appear mentally ill. Naturally, he took a good look at the man, and he remembers nothing remarkable about his behavior.

If you think about it, there's only one person who testified in this case who said he had known Hans Schroeder all during this period. That was Chief Goonan. And it was the only person who said in response to a question I asked him that at no time during this period, at no time, did Hans Schroeder fail mentally. We can put all the psychiatrists in the world up against a statement like that, and that won't make it false. I suggest to you he is extremely reliable. He is the chief of police in a town. He knows something about human nature. Part of his job is to observe human conduct. He knew Hans Schroeder, and he said that Hans Schroeder did not fail mentally during this period of acquaintance.

And I suggest to you that some of the other testimony in the case also supports our contention. Let's focus for a moment on Hans Schroeder's appearance and how he conversed on the way back from where he was picked up. He talked with Lieutenant Simmons, talked with Chief Goonan about the chief's son who is stationed in Baden Baden, Germany. Talked about his own service in the German army and how he was captured by the Russians on the Eastern front. Does this sound like somebody who is insane, someone who doesn't appreciate the criminality of his conduct?

Ladies and gentlemen of the jury, I ask you to believe the common sense testimony in the case. I ask you to apply your everyday experience to the testimony of Chief Goonan. To be sure, he didn't fail mentally during this period. Yes, he appeared to be worried. Sure, he was under some pressure. But, he didn't fail mentally.

Then we have the testimony of the psychiatrists. We have Dr. Barrows' testimony. The doctor did suggest that he was suffering from a psychotic depressive reaction, but not on November second. Indeed, it appears that it was the recognition of the enormity of his offense which precipitated this psychotic depressive reaction. Well, if that's true, if you believe Dr. Barrows' testimony, then the psychotic depressive reaction, even if it existed, had nothing to do with the offense. Why? Because the psychotic depressive reaction took place as a result of the offense, after he had done the deed. It was the enormity of what he had done — What did I do? What did I do? — that precipitated the psychotic depressive reaction.

I argue to you, ladies and gentlemen of the jury, that there never was a psychotic depressive reaction. This kind of disease can appear in a perfectly normal man, can get a grip on him at the time he commits a heinous act. And then, a few months later, a few years later, he's out again, happy as a bird, perfectly normal.

Dr. Mezer said, sure, he can hold down a job. He does. He holds down a job, goes to work every day. This so-called psychotic depression, isn't it a disease of convenience, if indeed it's a disease at all in this case?

You heard from Dr. Woodward. I submit to you that he's just as qualified as Dr. Mezer. And he said, no. In his opinion, this man never suffered from a psychotic depressive reaction. There simply weren't the things you'd normally see in a psychotic depressive reaction. Sure he was depressed, sure he was anxious. But there was no indication of any weight loss, no similarities to the kind of patients that Dr. Woodward has seen, where they come to his office and the wife has to answer all the questions. No. He didn't lose his job, but the psychotic depressive says, "Oh dear! do I still have my job?" Yes, you have your job; I called and it's okay. "Well, call up again and find out if I still have my job."

Dr. Woodward said that a man who's hopelessly in the throes of this depression can't take care of the normal functions of life. He becomes grossly impaired. But this man went out to work every day. On the day of the incident - or so he told the authorities and psychiatrists at Bridgewater - he went to a restaurant, got a raise in pay, he was going home to celebrate, to tell his wife about it. He had a couple of drinks at Ernie's. Nothing wrong with that. Does this present the picture of an insane individual? Or is it a person who may have had his difficulties, may have had his problems, may even have felt a terrible rejection at the hands of another woman, but he's certainly coping with his problems. He gets a raise in pay, he's going to tell his wife about it. Dr. Mezer said it was too little, too late, whatever he may have meant by that. I say to you

Hans Schroeder was functioning well within society. He knew what he was doing, and he appreciated the criminality of his conduct. He was perfectly capable, as Dr. Woodward has said, of conforming his conduct to the requirements of law.

The judge will tell you, far better than I can, that everybody is presumed to be sane. I didn't have to introduce any psychiatric testimony whatsoever. Of course, I do have to prove to you beyond a reasonable doubt that he was sane. That's part of my case. But I didn't have to put in any psychiatric testimony. Based on the other testimony that you've heard, including the defendant's own statements, his demeanour, his past history as he has recited it to other people, I submit you have enough material on which to decide that Hans Schroeder could appreciate the criminality of his conduct, that he could conform his conduct to the requirement of law.

But I went beyond that. I produced a psychiatrist. It's true the psychiatrist never examined the man. What is the point now? He's coming into the case years after the event took place. But based on experience, training, and education, he gave you a solid, reliable opinion. My brother, the defense, a highly skilled cross examiner, was unable to shake Dr. Woodward from his opinion that he did have this capacity, that he was in effect legally sane.

Now we've heard from Dr. Mezer, a highly qualified psychiatrist. I submit to you, as the defense pointed out, that you may quite truly accept testimony in this case from any individual, that you may reject in whole or in part any testimony presented before you. I argue that you should reject Dr. Mezer's testimony insofar as it relates to the opinion that this man did not have the requisite capacity we've been talking about.

Dr. Mezer testified at great length on direct examination, almost without interruption, and gave a detailed history. Went all the way back to the Eastern front, told us how the defendant made his way in this country, and the troubles that he had faced. And I asked him on cross-examination: "Dr. Mezer, have you given us all of the history in this case?" Yes, very complete, was what he said. I don't mean to misquote him, but he did say complete, in effect. And then I said to him, "Doctor, what about the statement that Hans Schroeder made to you that he had been seeing a woman for three and a half years?"

Now, I don't want to drag anybody else into this case. Enough people have been hurt. I certainly don't want to drag this woman's husband into the case. It is not part of the Commonwealth's case that the defendant was in fact having an affair with another woman. And I don't intend to prove it. There is no need to. But there was the recognition on the part of this defendant that he loved this other woman, regardless of whether he had a reason to or not. He loved this other woman, and because of it he intended to kill his wife and child. I asked Dr. Mezer this. He didn't remember at first. And I showed him something that refreshed his memory. And then he said, "Oh yes, I do remember it, having an affair for three and a half years with a woman, and her husband found out, and they had to call it off. The husband threatened Hans Schroeder. And then Mr. Schroeder became depressed. Oh yes, I do remember that now."

Ladies and gentlemen of the jury, should we place any substantial reliance on Dr. Mezer's opinion when he left out so important a piece of history? Why did he leave that out? Well, only you can answer that question. I submit to you he left it out because it didn't fit his nice little picture puzzle that he had already thought up in advance. He had decided well in advance, I submit to you: Oh sure, psychotic depressive reaction. Great defense. Sane man before, yeah, but perfectly, legally insane at the time of the crime. Oh, sure, can happen later on. Yeah, he can hold down a steady job and he's all right. Nice, neat defense to a murder. Couple it with amnesia, beautiful. But the irregular piece of the puzzle didn't fit into the picture. So Dr. Mezer discarded it. Left it out completely after he told us, yes, he was giving a complete history.

I submit to you, ladies and gentlemen of the jury, that Dr. Mezer's opinion is not to be relied upon in any substantial manner by you. Could he have lied to the psychiatrist? The defense brought out the possibility. Could he have conned you? Dr. Mezer was asked. Well, yes, anything is possible. Anybody can lie. How can you fake tears, how can you fake agitation? I asked the doctor if he had ever been to the movies. "Oh, well, yes, people cry in them. Oh, yes, people cry. People appear agitated. Oh, yes, but that's different." Or words to that effect. You remember what he said. I ask you, are we to rely upon that kind of opinion, totally discounting things which are unfavourable to the opinion and relying absolutely on things which support the opinion?

Indeed, Hans Schroeder's history is given to the doctor. Hans Schroeder doesn't remember the events, doesn't remember saying anything to the police officer which would indicate that he recognized responsibility for the act. Doesn't remember anything which, as the doctor said in his own words, was incriminating. Doesn't remember any of it.

I submit to you that he remembered it on November fifth when he said to Sanga, "I did it, I did it. I'm Hans Schroeder, the murderer." He remembered when he said to Goonan, "How can you be so nice to me after what I've done?" He remembered it when he said to Mrs. Constanza and to Ken Winters over the telephone, "I've just killed my wife and my child." He remembered it then. If this terrible disease had struck him as a result of Mrs. Constanza's rejection of him, then how did he manage to walk around normally for over a week or more? I suggest to you this defies imagination. If he was distraught and if he blacked out, and he couldn't remember this terrible deed because of the psychotic depressive reaction and amnesia, then how come he remembered it when he talked to Goonan, when he talked to Sanga and his fellow officers, when he talked to Ken Winters over the telephone, when he talked to Mrs. Constanza over the phone? Why is it that he remembers all of these things? And why is it that he didn't have amnesia when he wrote on the piece of paper which Sargeant Darsch found: "P.S. Ask Peggy, she can explain what it means." And there was a picture of Mrs. Constanza with an arrrow pointing to the words "I love you" over "Mein schwarzer kleiner teufel," my little black devil, followed by "P.S. Ask Peggy, she can explain what it means."

And then there were these words tagged on: "If anybody is looking for an answer, here is the answer. Only one person is responsible." Odd that he should've used the word 'responsible', isn't it? "And this is Mrs. Peggy Constanza," he writes.

I submit to you there is recognition of what he has done when he wrote the note. There is recognition of criminal responsibility. It's not amnesia. He remembered everything then. And then he ends the note, after mentioning a number of people, apparently friends: "Mein susser schwarzer teufel," my little black devil, "Ich liebe dich," I love you, and can't live without you, "dein liebling grune augen," Goodbye, my love, he signs it darling green eyes.

Did Hans Schroeder have amnesia when he wrote these words. Of course, he didn't, any more than he did when he made all those statements recognizing what he did, recognizing that what he had done was wrong. Ladies and gentlemen of the jury, there is no reliable evidence that should convince you that he lacked substantial capacity to conform his conduct to the requirement of law.

Dr. Mezer has said that a week before the incident, after the terrible rejection from Mrs. Constanza, he was at a point where he couldn't conform his conduct to the requirement of law. He was then a legally insane individual. And yet we see him carrying on with the normal functions of life. Here's a psychotic who, so the learned doctor says, can't conform his conduct to the requirements of law. But he's holding down a job, going to lunch with a couple of business associates, talking about a new job, going home, stopping off at another restaurant, having a couple of cognacs, a couple of beers. When he came home, he may have had another drink. That may or may not have been in evidence. Anyway, it's your memory that counts. And you'll remember testimony about a glass of anisette at home. Does this behavior suggest to you a man who is legally insane?

The defense made a good point when it pointed out that you don't go into the jury room and find yourself in a vacuum. You take with you everyday experience. You all possess the collective wisdom from different walks of life, from different and colourful backgrounds. I suggest to you this is infinitely more reliable than the opinion of a psychiatrist. The defense rightly pointed out that he couldn't tell, any more than you could, when a person was telling the truth and when lying. Take this experience, I submit to you, the history of the valuable experiences you've lived with all your lives. Take it into the jury room, and there decide. And I ask you to decide that Hans Schroeder was responsible, that he had the capacity to know what was expected of him, to conform his conduct to the requirement of law. He was not, by any stretch of the imagination, legally insane.

And now, ladies and gentlemen of the jury, I'm going to ask you to consider also the question of legal insanity. I use that word here as a shorthand, legal expression. The judge will no doubt explain what it is. But whenever I am using the phrase, I'm talking about the substantial capacity to conform his conduct to the requirements of law. That's what I'm implying when I use the words 'legal insanity'.

I ask you to consider on that question not only what he said, and all those times he said he did it and that he knew what he was doing, but also his actions.

I am referring particularly to the act of taking the bureau and positioning it as you may see from the photograph in evidence. This is the door to Katarina's room. The door is closed after the act. But here's the bureau which has been moved to block the front of the door. Does that imply purposeful conduct? He knew what he did was wrong, criminal, just as he knew it when he took the covers and placed them over the head of Katarina and over the head of his wife Eva.

Of course, he was sick when he was found in Connecticut. What normal person wouldn't be sick with this kind of burden weighing down on his conscience? The burden of the murder of one's wife and daughter. Of course, he's sick. Of course, he's distraught. What sane man wouldn't be? He had done a terrible thing and he knew it. That's why he was distraught. That's why he kept repeating, "I did it, I did it, I did it. I'm Hans Schroeder, the murderer. How can you be so nice after what I've done?"

I am going to ask you, ladies and gentlemen of the jury, to come in with a verdict of guilty of murder on both counts. And I am going to ask you to come in with a verdict of guilty of murder in the first degree, because this murder was committed with extreme atrocity and cruelty.

There are some pictures here, ladies and gentlemen, and some medical reports. You see them now, you'll see them at greater length later. I didn't put those pictures into evidence so as to inflame you against this man, or to provoke in you unreasonable emotional feelings towards him. I put them into evidence for one purpose and one purpose only. Assuming you found him to have killed these two women with malice aforethought, and assuming that you found him legally sane — and I submit to you 'yes' on both these questions — I want you to believe that he killed these women with extreme atrocity and cruelty. That, as the judge will explain to you, is murder in the first degree. That's why I put the pictures into evidence. That's why I put much of the pathological testimony into evidence. The wounds — yes, you'll remember the wounds from the axe — a blunt instrument cutting through not only the outer tissues, but the muscles as well, and even the bones. In several cases, the bone was fractured, splintered, and comminuted. You'll never forget that testimony, the evidence that we put in. And I did that only to show you how unspeakably violent the crimes were, how gruesome the murders.

It is on this basis that I ask you to come in with verdicts of murder in the first degree on both cases. I thank you very much.

13

⚜

"Look at yourself," said Eva. She thought I was a smaller man than she knew in Wiesbaden. But we only change in our dreams. In the morning we are back exactly where we were the night before.

I had this dream one night many years ago. I never discussed it with anyone, for who would understand? It was a crisp, cold night, but not so cold that people wouldn't venture outside. In fact, the moon was up and everything was bathed in silver. The men who walked at that hour, covered in quilted coats, looked like massive ponderous shadows, almost as large as the dark patches of buildings which were facing away from the light of the moon.

I suddenly caught sight of the German girl I had felt strangely drawn towards the day before. She was walking along the path on a level with the barrack, half hidden by a large snowdrift. One of the guard-tower searchlights swung spasmodically over her head, way over her head, and left her face in the darkness. As I lay staring outside through the glass-covered vent punched through the wall over my bunk, I couldn't help but notice several other shadows darting across the snow, from one patch of shadow to the other.

I remembered from the day before her wide face tied round with a red scarf whose ends fluttered behind her in the wind like the tail of a kite. Before she reached the bend in the path, the first shadow stepped out from behind the barrack and stood in her way. Tulla started and gave a short cry. Her cry was stifled right away as the shadow jumped at her throat, caught the back of her neck with one hand, and put the other over her mouth. Tulla bent back like a bow and raising her left leg from the ground pushed her knee into the attacker's stomach. At the same time, she grasped his beard with both hands and jerked the large fur-capped head away from her with all her strength. The shadow made a half circle with his left boot, and with a sharp kick knocked her right leg from under her. They both fell into the snowdrift together at the very moment when seven other men ran up from all directions,

They dragged her, holding her by the hands and legs, while her hair tumbled loosely behind, to the bottom of the hollow and threw her down on a snow-covered bench. They were about twenty five yards from the barracks. She met the first with a furious kicking of her legs, freed for a moment from her attacker's grasp. But soon she was quiet again, choked by the skirt which was thrown over her head, and Klevshin's enormous hand which he placed over her face, forcing her head down on the bench. I was certain it could be no one but Klevshin.

The first pinned her right leg to the back of the bench with one knee, and with his other leg pressed on the inside of the thigh which was hanging in mid-air and moving convulsively. While two others held her wrists, the first, half-kneeling, was tearing off her underclothes and calmly unbuttoning his trousers. After a moment, her body began to rock convulsively and

Klevshin had to loosen the grip of his fingers with each uneven jerk of her head. The second and third man had an easier task. Encouraged by the sudden calm of her body, the third impatiently dug for her breasts in the rumpled bundle of her skirt and blouse. But when it was the turn of the fourth, she managed for a moment to free her head from Klevshin's fingers. In the frosty silence, she let out a short, throaty cry, choking with tears and muffled by her skirt.

At the sound of the voice, the light from the nearest watchtower stopped in the midst of circling the eastern perimeter. A beam of light moved uncertainly for a moment and zeroed in on Klevshin and his men."C'mon fellows," cried a sleepy voice from the watchtower. "Do your thing somewhere else."

They pulled her off the bench, and, like a limp rag doll, dragged her behind the barracks to the latrine. I kept watching from the little window above my bunk, and found my body shivering in fear for the girl. After about an hour, the seven of them returned to the barracks. I saw Klevshin leading her back to the women's quarters. Tulla walked slowly, stumbling and tripping on the path, head drooping to one side, arms folded across her breasts, supported round her waist by the strong arm of her companion.

All around me was the night, thick and impenetrable, icy and menacing. A night without end and, worse, without hope. When the wind howled at night, it seemed to tell me that freedom wasn't for us. We were doomed to be chained to this little piece of Siberia for the rest of our lives. It mattered little that they didn't force us to wear chains. We could escape, we could wander away, but this vast, limitless waste was where we belonged, a home for doomed creatures.

Hunger turned us into animals. More than anything else, it was hunger that broke down the resistance of women. Once broken, it was downhill all the way. It sickened me to see how quickly women slid down to the darkest depths of sexual abandon. Some gave in not only with the hope of improving their conditions or finding a powerful protector, but also with the hope of maternity. Pregnant women in camps were freed from work for three months before and six months after the baby's delivery. Six months was the period considered sufficient for the suckling of a child until it was old enough to be taken away from its mother and transported to some unknown destination.

Tulla wandered about the camp till late at night like a cat on heat. Whoever wanted to, could have her, on a bunk, under the bunk if they craved some privacy, in the separate cubicles of the technical experts, or in the clothing store. Sometimes even on the sacks of potatoes in the potato store. Tulla delivered her baby in the heart of winter. During the last few months of her pregnancy, the urkas had more or less left her alone. They had other women to pursue. When one day I heard Klevshin and his men snickering among themselves about Tulla, about how they ought to get her back to work again, I knew she had probably had her baby. I didn't see her for a few more months. When I did catch sight of her early one spring morning, she was carrying her little baby in her arms. It filled me with immense joy to see them both. Tulla was looking beautiful. It was almost as if she had somehow renewed her youth through her child.

At first I brought her flowers. For some strange reason, flowers made the little girl's eyes water. That was when I decided to start making little figures for the baby. I picked up every piece of wood I found in the camp. I kept the pieces stowed away under my bunk, and carved little figures which I later coloured with paint one of the camp technicians kindly let me have. Everybody loved the baby, as did the technicians. Soon, they began to ask me to make figures and toys for them which they gave to Tulla as gifts for her baby.

During the day, especially when the sun was shining, we would crowd around Tulla and her baby as they sat on the steps to the women's barracks. Whenever the baby giggled, we all laughed uproariously. I never understood why.

Our moments of shared happiness didn't last very long. One morning in late summer, as we were playing around Tulla and her baby, I caught sight of Klevshin and some of his henchmen walking menacingly towards us. At first, he hovered around our circle, joining in our laughter. Then he quickly stepped inside and picked up the baby with both hands. A broad grin spread across his face as he said, "She has to go now. We're sending her to Leningrad tomorrow."

I will never forget the expression on Tulla's face, etched in pain and fury. She leapt up from the ground and lunged towards Klevshin. But his companions were quicker. They grabbed her roughly and pushed her back through the door of the barracks.

Tulla came to our barracks that night. Klevshin and his men were sitting around the fire, chatting. The rest of us were dozing in our bunks, some fast asleep already. Tulla fell at Klevshin's feet wordlessly. Then she began to sob uncontrollably and implored with him to give her back her baby. "We can give you another one if you want." Their poisoned laughter sent fear through my heart.

The girl slowly lifted herself off the ground. She straightened her arms, turned her head and looked at the man with loathing. Suddenly she raised her whole body and with the gleam of a mortally wounded animal in her eyes, spat straight in his face.

Klevshin sprang on her. She struggled for a moment and quietened down. Klevshin turned to the girl cowering in the corner, pulled his torn shirt round him, and through clenched teeth said in a voice which chilled my blood, "Lie down, you bitch, and off with your clothes. Be quick, or I'll choke the life out of you." Then he turned to his friends and said, "She's all for you."

First it had to be Klevshin. With only a smile and hardly any emotion, they took her one after the other. Tulla didn't offer any resistance this time, gently opening her thighs each time and even cupping her hands round the swinging buttocks over her. She didn't even whimper as their drunken hands crushed her small breasts. Then they opened the wooden door and pushed her noiselessly out of the barracks into the dark night outside.

There was something obsessive about the sight of Klevshin and the others preying upon Tulla's body. Strangely enough, deep inside I suppose I too wanted to prey upon her, but I imagined I could somehow raise it all to a nobler height with love and tenderness. There was a time when I felt an unshakeable faith in our innate nobility. We were capable of turning the basest acts into pure gold. It was our privilege, our rare magic, our elusive Rhinegold.

I opened my eyes and turned noiselessly towards my barbed wire window. My eyes followed Tulla as she lurched forward, stopped, and lurched again on her way to her barracks. Then she was one with the ashen grey that spread its wings outside.

But ah! the jury returns, and I haven't yet come to my dream. What I have been telling you about is a dream that keeps repeating itself so many times that I'm no longer sure of its beginnings. That was no dream surely. How strange to find a single chain linking dreams and real events in a circle, erasing all sense of beginnings and ends. Sometimes I find it impossible to tell which is real and which is the dream.

I catch myself beginning to tremble, more out of excitement than fear. Earlier in the day, I figured out the same explanation when the food had refused to go down my throat. There was something almost nauseous about it. A loud voice shakes me back to reality.

14

Mr. Foreman, to this indictment number 41052, what say you, is Hans Schroeder, the defendant at the bar, guilty or not guilty?

We find the defendant guilty of murder in the second degree.

Ladies and gentlemen of the jury, hearken to your verdict as the Court has recorded it. Indictment number 41052, you upon your oaths do say that Hans Schroeder is guilty of murder in the second degree. So say you, Mr. Foreman, ladies and gentlemen, so say you all.

Now, Mr. Foreman, to indictment number 41053, what say you, is Hans Schroeder, the defendant at the bar, guilty or not guilty?

We find the defendant not guilty by reason of insanity.

The Court wants to make it clear on the record the indictments, particularly the numbers of the indictments. 41052 is the indictment which charges the defendant with the murder of Eva Schroeder, and your verdict on that, Mr. Foreman and members of the jury, is guilty of murder in the second degree.

Indictment number 41053, in which the alleged victim was Katarina Schroeder, your answer is a verdict of not guilty by reason of insanity.

Ladies and gentlemen of the jury, hearken to your verdict as the court has recorded it. Indictment number

41053, you upon your oaths do say the defendant, Hans Schroeder, is not guilty by reason of insanity. So you say, Mr. Foreman, so, ladies and gentlemen, say you all.

Pat Piscitelli approached the bench. "Your Honour," he said, "number one, I would like to move for entry of judgement notwithstanding the verdict on the indictment on which Mr. Schroeder was found guilty, on the ground that it's an inconsistent verdict. Secondly, I would like the jurors to be polled as to the indictment upon which they have found him guilty. I ask that they be polled."

The jurors are polled individually, each one confirming the verdict of guilty of murder in the second degree. Then Pat Piscitelli moved to the bench once more.

"It seems to me," he said, "that if the Jury has found him to be insane at the time of these killings, there is no evidence as to who died first. The evidence is equally consistent with the fact that the daughter died first. If he was insane at that time and they each died within the span of a very short period of time, as the evidence clearly indicates, he could not have been sane when the second killing occurred. Not by any stretch of the imagination. Obviously, it's inconsistent."

It was going to be a frustrating afternoon for Pat Piscitelli. The court rejected his motion for entry of judgement notwithstanding the verdict, and then went about discharging the jury.

Mr. Foreman and members of the jury, including the alternates, both deliberating jury and the alternate jurors, you have had a long and arduous task. I am not

going to waste words with you. I know you have conscientiously sought to perform your duty to the best
of your abilities. No one can ask you more than that.
You are now free to go. You are discharged of your
duties. And if you haven't been paid, you may now
receive payment. The paymaster is in the building, so I
am informed.

The defense wanted to make an oral motion for a
new trial in view of the inconsistency in the verdicts.
If the jury found Hans Schroeder to be insane at the
time of the killings, obviously insanity must have carried throughout the time of the killings because, from
all the evidence heard, they occurred apparently at the
same time. But Judge Collins decided to wait for the
prosecutor to move for sentence.

The Clerk's voice rang through the clear New
England afternoon. Hans Schroeder, on indictment
number 41052, wherein you are charged with murder in the first degree of Eva Schroeder, the jury
having returned a verdict of guilty of murder in the
second degree, the court having considered the offense whereof you stand convicted, do order that
you suffer imprisonment for the term of your life,
and that this sentence be executed upon you and
within the limits of the Massachusetts Correctional
Institution, Walpole, and that you stand committed
to our common jail until removed in pursuance of
this sentence.

Judge Collins commented on the other indictment. On this, the statute is permissive, he said, as to
whether the defendant should be committed to any

mental institution for observation. As he understood the evidence in the case, there was no contention by anyone that Hans Schroeder was not now sane within the meaning of the law. The proper action of the court should be, he decided, to discharge the defendant on that indictment.

And so the Clerk announced. Hans Schroeder, on indictment number 41053, charging you with murder in the first degree of Katarina Schroeder, the jury having returned a verdict of not guilty by reason of insanity, the Court orders that you be discharged on this indictment.

Piscitelli began his arguments right away after the two-thirty recess. He hedged a little at first, asking for time to prepare an actual written motion. Then he decided to go ahead.

"First, your Honour, I should have technically filed a motion to prevent the entry or the filing of the verdict. I think I should have asked for a motion for arrest of judgement prior to recording. I hope I am covered by the motion I made for entry of judgement notwithstanding verdict. If not, I will now move to vacate the verdict which is filed and returned by the jury in the case involving Eva Schroeder."

Judge Collins denied the motion to revoke the imposition of sentence. Piscitelli continued, a smile lighting up his face for an instant. He was always so pleasant.

"Your Honour, on the motion for a new trial, I respectfully suggest that there has been an inconsistent verdict entered by the jury here. Very simply, there is no evidence before this court for the jury to determine who of Eva and Katarina died first. I have examined as much as I can of all the medical testimony we have before us. I find the evidence indicates that Dr. McBey, the chemist, testified that he found blood group O on the axe. But when he tried to group the blood of the two deceased he found that the daughter's blood was putrid. By that he means decomposed. In other words, blood grouping proved inconclusive.

"But Dr. McBey said he found the blood type of Eva as being blood group O. By inference then, it was Eva who survived and was the one who died second, if in fact Katarina's blood decomposed and became putrid. I assume you don't need an expert to say whichever decomposed first had obviously been dead the longer. You can infer that, but you can't infer that Eva died first. If anything, it clearly indicates that if you can find blood on the axe which can be grouped as O, and Eva's blood group is O, then Eva's must be the last body to be struck by the axe. I submit that the second body to be struck must be Eva's.

"If that is the case, and if the jury found him to be insane at the time, it's inconceivable that you can find these verdicts to be consistent. I believe there is general agreement that the insanity lasted over a period of time, and that the acts of Hans Schroeder from November 3 onwards seem to have been that of a mentally incompetent man.

"I have here Dr. Katsas' autopsy reports. Exhibit CC for identification."

AUTOPSY REPORT

Case A 66-115

Katarina Schroeder,
King Street
Kingston, Massachusetts

1. Multiple blunt injuries consistent (with axe wounds) with:
   a. Lacerations of face and scalp.
   b. Laceration of left hand and amputation of distal left thumb.
   c. Comminuted fractures of skull and facial bones.
   d. Subdural and subarachnoid hemorrhages.
   e. Lacerations of the brain.
2. Aspiration of blood, terminal.
3. Pulmonary congestion and edema.
4. Early postmortem changes.

OPINION

It is our opinion that Katarina Schroeder came to her death as a result of multiple blunt injuries consistent (with axe wounds) with comminuted fractures of the skull and face and lacerations of the brain. Homicide.

Signed by the Medical Examiner and Pathologist.

POSTMORTEM EXAMINATION OF THE BODY OF
Katarina Schroeder

The following marks and injuries are on the body:

1. A gaping wound, 6 cm. long, between the inner canthus of the eyes and through the bridge of the nose with comminuted fracture of the nasal bones.

2. Bluish discoloration and swelling of the eyelids of both eyes, more pronounced on the medial part.

3. A gaping wound, 5 cm. long, transversely on the left side of the forehead.

4. A gaping wound, 6.5 cm. long on the left fronto-temporal area at the hairline.

5. A gaping wound, 12 cm. long, on the left temporo-occipital area of the head above the left ear. The skull bone is fractured beneath wounds #2, #3, and #4, with exposure of the intracranial cavity and its contents.

6. A gaping wound, 14 cm. long, on the left cheek from the nose to the ear with linear abrasions and lacerations extending from its margins on to the face. This wound extends on the auricle of the left ear with focal disruption of the cartilage.

7. Traumatic amputation of the distal phalanx of the left thumb.

8. A deep wound, 3 cm. long, on the left thenar with deep laceration of the soft tissues between the first and second metacarpal bones.

9. A gaping wound, 8 cm. long, on the dorsum of the left hand overlying the second, third, and fourth metacarpal bones with laceration of underlying muscles and tendons.

10. A superficial wound, 2 cm. long, on the dorsum of the left hand over the fifth metacarpal bone.

"And now Exhibit DD for identification."

AUTOPSY REPORT

Case A 66-114

PATHOLOGICAL DIAGNOSES ON THE BODY OF

Eva Schroeder

King Street

Kingston, Massachusetts

1. Blunt force injury of the head, with:
   a. Gaping wound of right temporal area and right eye.
   b. Comminuted fracture of the skull.
   c. Subdural and subarachnoid hemorrhages.
   d. Laceration of the brain.
   e. Retro-orbital hemorrhage, right.
2. Aspiration of blood, terminal.
3. Pulmonary congestion and edema.
4. Early postmortem changes.

OPINION

It is our opinion that Eva Schroeder came to her death as the result of blunt force injury of the head consistent (with blow with axe) with fracture of the skull and laceration of the brain. Homicide.

Signed by the Medical Examiner and Pathologist.

POSTMORTEM EXAMINATION OF THE BODY OF

Eva Schroeder

HISTORY: The deceased, a 44-year old married white female was found dead in her bed on November 4,

1966. A large amount of blood was present about the head.

AUTOPSY: The examination includes autopsy and was performed in the Faithful Shepherd Funeral Home, Pembroke, Massachusetts, beginning at 4:00 p.m., November 4, 1966. The examination was performed by William C. Gould, M.D., Medical Examiner, 214 Main Street, Kingston, and George G, Katsas, M.D., Pathologist, 130 Prince Street, Jamaica Plain.

EXTERNAL EXAMINATION: The body is that of a white female, measuring 161.5 cm. (63.7 inches) in length and weighing an estimated 110 pounds. The body is dressed in a nightgown and panties. A wedding band and diamond ring are on the left ring finger. The face and hair are covered with blood. There are bloodstains on the upper extremities. The hair is brown with grey streaks. The eyes are blue with cloudy aclerae and hemorrhage in the right eye. The right pupil measures 5 mm. in diameter and the left 4 mm. There is displacement of the left eyeball in the socket. Rigor mortis is absent. There is posterior dependent lividity. The vaginal temperature taken at approximately 5:30 p.m. is 70 degrees Fahrenheit. The teeth are natural. There is suntan throughout the skin surface except for the areas corresponding to a two-piece bathing suit. There is early postmortem change with greenish discoloration of the skin on the left lateral aspect of the chest and abdomen. The oral and nasal cavities contain blood.

There is a gaping, sharp edged wound, 10 cm. long, on the right temporal area a little above the ear to the upper right eyelid. The intracranial cavity and its contents are exposed in the depth of the wound. There is bluish swelling of the eyelids of both eyes, more pronounced in the right.

"I have checked out these autopsies and there is not one bit of evidence in either indicating who died first. There are almost identical words describing the condition of the bodies, but no evidence to suggest that Eva died first. If in fact you can infer that Eva died first, then I suppose you might argue that the verdicts are consistent. But if not, then there's no way these verdicts can be upheld.

"I have checked out some law concerning this. If I may, the oldest case in Massachusetts that I can cite is the case of Commonwealth versus Haskins, at 128 Massachusetts, page 60. This dealt with a larceny case, larceny of a car and receiving stolen goods. In that case, the court said, 'You cannot be found guilty of both.' It states on page 62: 'The record showed a verdict so inconsistent and uncertain in law that no judgement could be entered upon it.'

"While there are many cases on what constitutes an impermissibly inconsistent verdict I would cite a principle which states: 'In criminal cases, no form of verdict will be good which creates a repugnancy or an absurdity in a conviction.' I suggest that is what we have here.

"We have also found some cases dealing with similar situations where a man kills his wife and then kills someone else and raises the defense of insanity. In each one of those cases, the indications are upon the evidence that the man had killed his wife in a fit of anger or passion and then, because of it, shot some other people. And the court said that the jury could find that he was guilty of the murder of his wife and then, in a fit of anger, hatred, or jealousy, he then became insane when he killed the others. Those two verdicts are obviously consistent.

"But that's not the case here. You have sheer guesswork on the part of the jury as to which one of the bodies was in fact killed first. Everything indicates, from the autopsy to Dr. McBey, everything suggests that Eva Schroeder could have died first.

"And with the hair on the axe. Why was this not tied in? We don't know whose hair it was or what was its colour. All the indication we have is that some hair was found on the head of an axe. While the hair of the two parties is different, we can't tell whose hair it was on the axe. The verdict, your Honour, is equally consistent with Katarina having been killed first, as it was with Eva. That being the case, the man could have been insane when Katarina was killed, which the jury said he was. It would be absurd to say that he suddenly had a moment of lucidity, or rationality, and then killed Eva. That would seem to fly in the face of common sense.

"I am asking, your Honour, for a stay of execution of sentence. Hans Schroeder has been out on $25,000 bail since August 22, 1972. He has been here throughout the course of almost three weeks of the trial. With all due deference to the court's opinion, I respectfully suggest that there are serious questions which might constitute reversible error. This is my third murder case before your Honour, and I have great respect for your judgement. But there are very serious questions in this case, all of them could be legitimate grounds for reversal of this case.

"This man is not going anywhere, your Honour. So if your Honour thinks there is some basis or some merit to my numerous exceptions, then I respectfully ask that you allow the man to remain out. Set a bail. Set a high bail. I think $25,000 is high enough in this case. And allow us to pursue our appeal immediately, as we intend to. I feel quite confident that justice will better be served if the execution in this case is stayed."

Mr. Concannon was overruled. Judge Collins granted the motion for stay of execution. The Clerk announced in his powerful voice, "Hans Schroeder. On Indictment number 41052, the Court orders execution of said sentence be stayed pending the final determination of appeal. The Court orders that you be admitted to bail, and the bail is the same as it presently is."

15

I woke up early next morning with a sudden start. I felt frightened by the surrounding darkness, the unaccustomed stillness. At Walpole, I had trained myself to sleep right through a dozen TVs and radios, all tuned to different stations, sometimes blasting away into the wee hours of the morning when the guards forgot to turn the power off. For years now, when I woke up it was not because my body had all the rest it craved, but because some terrible scream or hellish clatter shattered my sleep and made my flesh creep in fear. It happened all the time. But today, my body seemed surprised by a new situation. It had had its fill, undisturbed. I felt surprised by peace, exhausted by an unexpected silence.

It is not as if this was my first night in my mother's house. I had come straight to this house the day I was granted parole. It looked sadder than I remembered six years ago. I didn't ask Mother where Chris, Dennis and Carolyn were. She didn't bring up the subject either. To this day she hasn't. I think it is better this way.

Yesterday, the rapid turn of events had been too sudden, too terrifying. As I sat in the cell adjoining the courtroom, I had found a lot of time to think of many things. When the guard returned to summon me back to the courtroom, my first reaction was less of disappointment than fear. My legs seemed to give way momentarily at the thought of returning to Walpole, but the question of my guilt or innocence never crossed my mind.

I was certain it was all over for me. I wasn't sure where Piscitelli was leading me to. There were times I felt that I ought to have persisted with Homans. As a lawyer, Homans was a powerful guy with a big reputation. I suppose it was natural he would take a little longer to reply to my request for taking up the case. I was angry with myself for not having waited a few more weeks, for having listened to prison talk and gone along with Piscitelli. Sure, the man had found a lot of luck successfully defending five Norfolk prison murderers one after the other. But I was no prison murderer. The thought did cross my mind that I had been conned once more.

Come to think of it, Walpole wouldn't have been unbearable to me any more. Alone in my prison cell, what I seemed to want most of all was company. Someone alive, someone to talk to, someone to taunt and tease. In the beginning, it was this about my punishment I dreaded most. Gradually, it seemed a punishment well deserved. In the eyes of the law, I know I'd be crazy to even think of human companionship, especially after what they said I had done. But surely, I had not lost the right to new friendships. That's where Harry came in, our secret friendship.

Yes, there is no fairness in prison. There were others around me who had maimed but not killed, robbed but not maimed. They were being punished just like me. This is not fair, I said to myself. As the years passed, I was surprised how much sympathy I began to feel for others on my block. And then, all too sudden, hell would raise its head.

I had been accustomed to seeing blacks as blurs against a white background. But within the walls of the prison, the blurs took on shapes. Suddenly, I became aware of bodies, bodies bruised and kicked around, black, shining, bloodied bodies. Suddenly, there were people with feelings all around me, black and white, goaded by the guards to quivering rage.

All that now seems like one more dream. I can hear Mother pottering around the house just like Grandma used to. It breaks my heart when she looks at me. For her I will always remain what I was in 1939, a tall, blond, rather frail-looking young man in his late teens. I still have blue eyes and a large head, but no longer the face that was once on the whole rather handsome in a pink-cheeked way, not particularly sensitive and not particularly strong. I don't know what she sees in my face, but I am all dried up and twisted inside.

I had another dream last night. Of late, I seem to be floundering in an ocean of dreams. They will be my undoing, I think. They creep into my mind when I least expect them. They come tumbling out of nowhere, all jumbled and confused.

Last evening, when I was having supper with Mother, it all came back to me, the evenings of my childhood. Yes, when dusk approached, it was time to draw up the chairs around the old wood stove. I could see my mother preparing the evening meal, boiling water, all on the stove. Grandma was never far away from the stove. She was convinced that her blood would freeze at a distance of more than eight feet away. As soon as the warmth touched her insides, Grandma dozed off in her rocking chair. As the clock struck each hour, the fire died a little, and the room grew colder. One by one, folks would head for their rooms and return with a coat, a heavy wrap, or a second pullover. Nobody really wanted to move away from their favorite spot, for there was no heat in the other rooms. When the time came to retire for the night, one took possession of whatever comforts one could - hot water bottles, blankets, and warm underwear.

And when the first snowflakes fell on the crabapples no one had bothered to pick, I loved the white crowns over the glistening colours of the ripe fruit. Then the sun rose in the sky and melted the crowns. It was a ceaseless source of wonder to me to wake up on some mornings and find the colours exactly as I loved them, knowing it would all be different in a few weeks. Each day it was a little different. The colours darkened and, though the snow fell often, the shine and the radiance were no more. By January, the fruits that still clung to the branches were withered, their colour a dark, leathery brown.

My dreams will not let me be. Let me tell about the one I was going to before I was interrupted by the jury. I was in my bunk in Yercevo, fast asleep. It was midnight. Around me, enveloping me in a strange peace, there began the strange nightly progression of noises. First a snore, then whistling breaths and painful moans, low at first, then growing louder into an almost continuous lament broken only by occasional convulsions of dry, tearless sobbing which shook the prisoners on their bunks. Someone would shout violently, someone else would wake up from his sleep and sit up, warding off invisible attackers with hands outstretched. Others woke up, looking around unconsciously with an oblivious gaze, then quickly regaining consciousness and lying back with a profound sigh. The sleep-laden, disjointed babblings formed themselves into a sustained chorus begging to get out of hell.

The prisoners tossed and turned anxiously on their bunks and clutched at their hearts in sudden spasms of fear. Their limbs and bodies often thudded against the hard planks and woke me up with a start. Some nights, I would find it impossible to go back to sleep. I spent hours staring in the dim light of the fire at the tangle of bodies caught in the web of the night.

On that particular night, I was thinking of the work detail I had been engaged in over the past few weeks. My hands were blistered, my limbs ached constantly. We were digging a canal. It was a wide band of dark earth through the white snow. Its sixty feet width had to be dug down to a depth of twenty feet. Our implements were picks, primitive shovels we used for clearing snow, and wheelbarrows so antiquated they would've served museums better. Our predecessors had reached a depth of nine feet to expose the arctic permafrost, leaving us with a task more impossible than formidable.

As October came to an end, the last lights disappeared over the horizon quickly. Then the polar night began, lasting till the end of January. Sunrise disappeared at the beginning of the polar night. Only around noon did the sun appear briefly, like a false dawn swiftly gone. Each day this interlude of light grew shorter and shorter. Then began the period of total darkness. This is the beginning of the polar night which lasts for three months. In December the terrible dark purga began to rage. It blew and rested, then blew again.

At the end of January, one could see the daylight in the south for brief moments. It was a sign that the polar night would soon draw to a close. To the mute world of the Arctic, this heralded the return of sunlight. Slowly, and by degrees, the light increased in duration. The dawn lasted longer until the appearance of the first golden rays of true sunlight. It was in this manner that spring crept into the Arctic. In its wake came the brief summer.

I always felt a little better about the camp in the summer than at other times. Yercevo wouldn't have won any prizes, but it seemed an infinitely better camp than the others I had known or heard about. They said it was a little more human here. At least, no numbers on one's clothes, so we called out to each other by our names. And that was what I liked most about the summer. People called out to one another a lot more than at other times. We spent more time outside, since this was the only real time to get work done. There were holes to be dug, roads to be levelled, barbed wire to be laid down, and sheds to put up. The cold sunlight thawed the earth to a depth of twelve inches or so. The pickaxes bounced off the permafrost a little later than at other times.

While the camp inmates worked up enormous appetites in the summer, the quality of camp food was usually at its lowest during this time of the year. By July, the stock of the previous year's vegetables was usually coming to an end. While there was some sense of welcome relief after six months of cabbages or salted carrots, there was also the constant possibility of such surprises as shredded nettle soup or gruel with floating fish eyes. Only the black bread and potatoes remained the same from day to day, year after year. Another staple was hvoya, a dark-green infusion of pine needles we drank to avoid vitamin deficiency.

From the beginning of May until July - for three months - the sun did not set. It created a whiteness which covered everything. But it was a cold light. Some flowers bloomed in an explosion of colours in the tundra. Small plants, hiding from the cold winds, they barely rose above the ground. Although the blossoming did not last more than two or three days, every variety of grass and weed suddenly came to life.

When these were gone, there returned the snow and ice, darkness and the grey tundra, thick fog and stormy waters. The unrelenting cold, harsh winds, and death came back to haunt us with a dogged determination.

At times, when the polar night had settled down, one saw in the dark, star-spangled skies the northern lights shimmering with colours which rose and fell like shattered rainbows. Even the full moon appeared much larger than I could ever remember. At times, it reminded me of an enormous lamp shaded by the boundless white waste which spread all around me.

But it's Tulla I wanted to tell you about. It was past midnight when she crept into our barracks. Klevshin and his men were sprawled around the fire, snoring. Tulla went and squatted in front of the fire, warming her hands. I saw her with a stake I had fashioned with my tools because she had wanted me to. She stuck this in the fire while she sat warming herself in front of it. I must have dozed off. When I opened my eyes, I saw Tulla standing in front of the sleeping Klevshin. Her hands were raised above her head. She was clutching the stake in her hands, its sharpened end glowing red hot from the fire.

I knew what Tulla was up to. I wanted to help her, to hold her hands and drive the stake through Klevshin's heart. But I couldn't move. In the end, Tulla went through the cleansing sacrifice herself. With a smile on her face, she brought the stake down and pierced Klevshin's heart. He gave a blood chilling scream which I knew to be the last sound he would ever make.

Tulla ran away into the night. Once they understood what had happened, Klevshin's men gave chase. They never found her.

But we did, early next morning when the mist lay heavy over the barracks and the air was damp and cold. It was at a point quite the opposite of the one in which the guards and Klevshin's mates had run in search of her. Somehow she must have circled round the long camp perimeter, hiding from the lights, hiding behind banks of snow, until the wind blew away the telltale signs of her footprint and they lost her. There was something stunning and unexpected about the discovery. We were on our way to resume digging the canal next morning. This was a spot I had not been assigned to in the past. I moved through the thick mist not knowing where I was going, led by others who knew the way. After a while, I thought I could see some light and wondered if it could be the glow that I had seen from my bunk on clearer nights. A fellow worker told me yes, this was the glow one could see from the barracks. They set fire to old tires to soften the ground for the shovels the next day.

We came upon a pit surrounded by low coils of barbed wire. Even from a distance I could see what looked like Tulla's red scarf caught in the strands. My heart beat faster. Could it be she was somewhere out there, huddled beside the fires for warmth. There was a wide circle of burning tires immediately below the edge of the pit. A few feet away from the row of tires was a large rock which the workers had been unable to move away. I wept when I caught sight of Tulla. She must have rushed headlong through the barbed wire and plunged onto the rock below. We found her lying on the rock like a wilted flower, her neck broken from the fall. It was all surprisingly clean, very little blood on the rock.

That was no dream. That was real. I would lie on my bunk on many a night afterwards, full of shame. My fellow prisoners slept in the oppressive silence of the barrack the feverish sleep of those in pain, sucking the air with a whistle through half-opened lips, turning restlessly from side to side, gabbling and sobbing in their sleep in a heart-rending whisper. I remained awake, tormented.

In the past, my own dreams were often erotic and cannibalistic in the extreme. Love and hunger seemed to return to their common biological origins, releasing from the depths of the subconscious images of women made of fresh dough whom I would bite in fantastic orgies until blood and milk sprang out of them as if from a fountain, their arms smelling of fresh loaves entwined around my burning head. I would wake up, exhausted and covered in sweat, usually when the Moscow-Archangel Express sped like an arrow of sound each night, at about the same time, a mile or so away from our camp.

From the day Tulla died, my midnight dreams were always of her standing on top of the sleeping Klevshin. Every night, I would push myself to rise up and help her. Every night I would fail. Every night I would be too late. I think I succeeded only once, the night Eva and Katarina died. Oh my God!

Katarina. Katarina. The name was music to my ears whenever anyone called out her name. Katarina and I. I and Katarina. The more intensely I loved her the more I was haunted by dark fears and shame, by shadows of suspicion. At times I grew fearful of the shadows, and that was when my love for her took on an air of desperation. I often wondered if I was right to love my daughter the way I did. Eva said she found it amusing, and rather odd.

Eva and I. Our love died somewhere along the way. It is not supposed to, but it does. It did. At first, it probably started with small differences, a question of taste, a question of timing. Much of it was in silence, like pretending to have overlooked something you never wanted to do anyway. Then one day the silence became too much for one or the other. Then started the questions, the accusations, the blame. All the while, the children were growing up, the groceries needed to be hauled in day after day, visits to doctors and dentists, clothes to be purchased and laundry that must be taken care of - all the crap that gets in the way of seeing things as they truly are. We never realized we were falling out of love. We looked at objects and situations with reason, and found all sorts of reasons except the real one, the one that said love was no more.

But I continued with Katarina. That too was a way of not facing up to the truth. Katarina was growing more and more beautiful by the day. I thought I wanted to shape her life. In truth, I wanted to run her life. In truth, I wanted to be a part of her life. It sounds silly, but I never figured out what it might all add upto. Perhaps that's because I'm not after all a man of reason. So when Katarina returned from a trip to the whaling museum in New Bedford one day and declared she was prepared to give up piano for skrimshaw I for one saw nothing wrong with it at first. Eva was scornful and angry at the suggestion. The more I thought about it the more skeptical I too became. I thought it wouldn't be the same in the evenings, not to hear the sound of her music which I had been preparing myself for from the moment I left work.

But the next morning it seemed a wonderful idea all over again. I began to see scrimshaw much the same way as I once saw my toys - expressions of love, paths into the hearts of children and grownups alike. It thrilled me inwardly to see Katarina's thoughts developing in a way not too different from mine.

16

I met Hans in Ernie's Diner later that afternoon. For months, this was the place where men had debated the fate of Hans Schroeder. They had done so once before, at the time of the first trial. Then the discussions moved along to other subjects - the war, jobs, sanitation, schools, blacks. The new trial had reopened the subject with all the passion, insight, and prejudice the men of Brockton could muster.

There were those who had known Hans. There were those whose wives had known Eva. There were those whose daughters were friends of Katarina. Some days, the arguments heated up to the point where friends became sullen at each other. On other days, folks seemed torn between what they were hearing and what their wives or children had led them to believe. None of this probably touched Ernie, who had known Hans all along. Serene in the knowledge that all these little animosities, irritations and indignation would give way to other issues waiting in the wings, Ernie continued to dish out his bacon and eggs in the morning, burgers and beans in the afternoons, and whatever else you wanted at supper time, with his strong special coffee brewing all the time, all night and all day it seemed.

I had reported on the courtroom proceedings from the very beginning. As I waited for Hans to show up for our meeting, I could hear the excited conversation all around me. Everyone seemed to have a view on whether justice had been done or whether it had miscarried as usual. Of course, everyone was full of admiration for Pat Piscitelli. But there were some who felt sorry for Concannon. May be they knew him personally, may be they thought he stood for justice and the right cause. Piscitelli was known for going to bat for lost causes. This won him many clients, but also detractors who were scornful of his good looks and his Mercedes.

From time to time, someone would ask my views on the subject. "He never got what he deserved, did he?" someone asked. I was in no mood to join in the conversation. I looked at the flowered plastic covering on the table, the soiled ashtrays, the ketchup, the salt, the pepper and the sugar and wondered how long I was destined to cover this beat. The story of Hans Schroeder seemed so mean and so trivial, not unlike the lives most of us in the diner led. I had seen it from day to day. It was my job to write about the trial from day to day. Suddenly, I was amazed at how little I knew about the man. All I knew about him was through the eyes of others, the police, the psychiatrists, the attorneys. Still, what little I knew I felt compelled to present to the town's audience. For their pleasure, their enlightenment?

All conversation stopped a little after six. I knew Hans had walked in through the door. Then, unexpectedly, someone began to clap his hands softly, slowly. Before long, another person joined in, then another. Soon the diner shook with the collective applause of its patrons. I found myself doing the same, quite unconsciously. One by one, several of the men walked over to Hans and shook his hand. Hans just stood there, tears rolling down from his eyes.

"What are you trying to do to me?" asked Hans. "You know, I'm grateful for all your help, but I'm innocent. That's the judgement I'd pass on myself today if I could, if it meant anything." I stared at him, puzzled.

"I know what you're thinking. I know what some of the others in Ernie's must be thinking. That I was such a nice guy, must've flipped or something. Could happen to anyone, huh?" I nodded in silence.

"What you saw and heard in the courtroom wasn't my story."

"What do you mean?" I asked.

"A story is like a toy, much like the wooden toys I used to make. You whittle away at the wood with a knife, and little by little a face, a figure begins to show. Meanwhile, on the floor below lies a scattered pile of wood shavings and pieces of wood. Are they not part of the toy? What would the toy be without the wood chips on the floor? Nothing."

"Nothing?" I asked.

"Nothing."

I looked down at my lukewarm cup of coffee incredulously. "Let me explain," Hans continued. '"You heard them come up with a story of a man who had brutally killed his wife and daughter with an axe. They hacked away at my sanity, my decency, my dignity, all the love I ever felt for Katarina and Eva, till it all lay like garbage strewn on the floor. But that wasn't it. What they told you in court wasn't the real story. I have inherited the garbage. That's as much part of the real story as anything else. Wotan is nothing without Brunnhilde, nothing without Siegfried. See?

"As I stepped into the forest I found myself surrounded by whispered sounds until suddenly there came blasts from an unseen horn - perhaps Siegfried's - that seemed to build up my confidence with every step I walked over the damp, fallen leaves, vaguely expecting to stumble across some glorious apparition. That was the kind of person I was. We set out to conquer the world and ended up grovelling for food. But you know, no matter what happened I could never shake off the music that held me spellbound in my youth as I sat on the silent steps at the back of the Wiesbaden opera house. Tell me, have you ever loved someone today and not cared if the world came to an end tomorrow?'

"I don't know," I said.

"I felt that way about Peggy," he said. "Or was it Tulla?" he asked distractedly.

"Will you gather up the garbage and place it in my hands?" I asked. "So I can make out the truth."

"Yes, but you can't mix my garbage with Piscitelli's. I don't think I could do it either. I don't think anyone can. Each pile is separate, distinct."

After a long pause when both of us said nothing, when everyone in Ernie's had become unnaturally silent, Hans began. "Through the window over my head the world made no sense at all ....

It was well past ten when we realized the diner was empty but for Ernie. He sat behind the counter near the cash register, thumbing through some magazine or the other, too polite to interrupt us or ask us to leave. "I'll tell you more later," said Hans. "We must let Ernie return to his wife and kids." Ernie just smiled, too tired to come up with a retort which he normally would have ready at the tip of his tongue. We left the diner and went our separate ways.

Late into the night, I worked on my column for the Brockton Enterprise. Even as I was starting to understand Hans, I found myself drifting into my own uncertainties. Obsessive longing, a lost love, shame and helplessness - together, what awesome goals they goad us to? I could not see how the law could ever disentangle these threads once they melt into the one compulsive, terrifying stroke of the axe. How could the law understand it all?

Finally, I started to come up with something which struck me later as totally irrelevant. In next morning's copy of the newspaper, I said there were still tears staining his cheeks and his eyes were red as Hans Schroeder walked to his car parked near the Belmont Street courthouse Thursday shortly before 4:00 p.m. It wasn't a walk Schroeder was supposed to take. But he was taking it.

Less than three hours earlier, he had been sentenced in Brockton Superior Court to life imprisonment for the November 2, 1966, axe-slaying of his wife. It didn't really come as a shock to him. He'd heard the words "for the term of your natural life" once before, in 1968, when he was convicted of the murders of both his wife and daughter.

An appeals court had reversed that decision and, for the last three weeks, Schroeder had been on trial again. No matter what a man has done, a long trial is an ordeal, and it took its toll on Schroeder. Periodically, he broke down, He was unable to sleep at night, and his eyes were already red from that lack of sleep when he came to court in the morning.

He had little appetite and his ulcer kicked up. Instead of going out for lunch at the noon recess, he usually took long walks. Through it all, though, he stood up and his concern was directed towards his mother.

"It is hard on her," he said, through his still thick German accent. "She never knows if I'll be coming back or not."

Once during the trial, there was talk of "copping a plea". His attorney, Pat Piscitelli, told him they might get prosecutor Brian E. Concannon to agree to let him plead to a lesser charge than the first degree murder he was being tried for. He might well be out in a year. But even though he knew he would automatically be sentenced to the electric chair if convicted of first-degree murder, he refused to even discuss pleading to a lesser charge.

"I just don't know if I did it," he told his attorney. "I loved them very much." While Schroeder wasn't sure, the jury was when it began its deliberations. The only thing they weren't sure was whether he was sane when he did it.

The knotty question tied up the nine men and three women for over thirteen hours and, when they did return a verdict, they still hadn't resolved the question. The jury found Schroeder guilty of second-degree murder in the slaying of his wife but not guilty by reason of insanity of the murder of his daughter.

Judge Joseph K. Collins, sitting on his last criminal case before retiring, sentenced Schroeder to the mandatory life sentence for the second-degree murder conviction. He discharged Schroeder on the other one.

Piscitelli immediately moved for a new trial and a stay of execution of sentencing which the judge said he'd consider later in the afternoon. As the sheriffs led Schroeder away, he was convinced, as was his attorney, that he would sleep in Walpole Prison that night.

Shortly after 3:00 p.m., Judge Collins heard Piscitelli on his motions. Piscitelli argued long and hard that the verdicts were inconsistent and therefore Schroeder deserved a new trial. Judge Collins denied the motion.

Piscitelli then argued that Schroeder should be freed pending appeals because there were, he felt, several errors which might be grounds for a reversal. He had made over one hundred and forty exceptions during the trial.

Concannon argued that the conviction was just and sentencing should not be stayed. Judge Collins paused a moment and then showed the rare quality that has made him one of the finest Superior Court judges sitting. He admitted he may have been wrong.

"I'm granting your motion, Mr. Piscitelli," said the white-haired jurist. "There are some serious questions that have to be answered by other courts."

There was a stunned silence. Concannon looked as if somebody had slapped him in the face. Piscitelli froze, then broke into a smile. Schroeder's legs got rubbery and he shed tears of relief. He was taken by the deputies to get his possessions.

And then he walked out onto Belmont Street.

17

I met Hans again the next day. "Have you nothing to tell me about Peggy?" I asked.

A strange look came over Hans. It was a mixture of amusement and contempt. This soon gave way to an indescribable sadness.

They think Peggy is a part of my crazy imagination, he said, an invention of my fantasies. All the shrinks think that way, and I'm sure you do too, he added.

I liked my little corner in the appliance and hardware store. I looked at each customer and wondered how much it takes some people to make money and how easy it is for others. As a child, a young man more likely, I am certain I dreamt of wealth and money. But it was something my friends and I would share, a collective wealth which was lying somewhere waiting for us.

One day I was startled by a loud clatter of objects falling, followed by a muffled cry of pain. It was a woman's voice. The woman had slumped onto the floor. A plastic basket had slipped off the shelf and now lay upturned over her shoulders, covering her head. I ran over to where she lay propped against the shelf and gently lifted the bucket off her head. A flood of dark lustrous hair tumbled out of the bucket. If I felt a pang of disappointment over the hair being black instead of gold, it left me as soon as I had sensed the unusual beauty of the oval face and the smooth, browned complexion. I fell in love with that face in an instant, and I think she with me. Now they tell me it was all in my imagination. Lies, lies, lies. It was like Brunnhilde's awakening. There was music in the air. And I heard it.

Yes, Tulla came to me when I was least expecting her. Another time, I remember her walking into the appliance store one sultry afternoon. She looked so delicate, so ethereal, framed against the rain splashing down our store window. I had no toys for her, no flowers. But I gave her what she needed, what I had.

I knew it was a challenge to my passions when she returned again a few months later, this time to work by my side. In another time, another place, I would have soared into the skies at her bidding, would've darkened the sun with my passion, melted the moon with my tenderness. But here I am, shackled to what I've been told a thousand times is reality. What is reality? It is everything that is mean. Everything that is cowardly.

I will not buy this reality, though I know my chains are real. I have felt their cold, inhuman touch. I have seen them bite into my flesh.

Even if one were to keep love completely out of it, the humor of our first meeting soon gave way to the ways of business, if you know what I mean. Like working side by side in the appliance store, talking about the sales reps, staying wary of the rip-off artists. Then she invited me home one day where I met Timmy for the first time. That's when I found out her husband had left her for another woman.

Timmy liked little things, she told me. So I began to prepare myself to carve something out for him. But then Timmy liked little things like eyelashes. All day in school, and at home too, he played with his eyelashes, flicking them, smoothing them over with his fingers. Other children teased him about this. They all did. He didn't have a single friend. They called him weird, jabbed their fingers in his body, pushed him around. When their teasing got too much for him, his eyes became small and frightened. I saw this in school one day. That's when he would throw his head from side to side as if searching, looking for a quick escape. Eventually, he would simply stand there, grow still, and wet his pants. After that, the taunting and the laughter seemed to mean nothing to him. He had retreated into his own little world.

It so happened Timmy was in Denny's class. I tried to reason with Dennis, telling him how much Timmy needed a solid friend, that it didn't matter he was a little odd. My heart went out to Timmy, and for three years I tried so hard to break into his world, to try and make some sense out of it. Of course, I was in love with Peggy. Eva knew full well I was seeing her. But I was seeing her as much for herself as for Timmy. I could never make Eva understand this.

There was a haunting, far-away look in Timmy's eyes when he was not defending himself or looking frightened. Sometimes it seemed a dark and angry look, far too angry for a nine-year old kid. There were other children in Denny's class one wanted to reach out to, tell funny stories, share one's thoughts, or simply pass on words of advice. With Timmy it was just the opposite. His wild, brown eyes scared people, pushed them into corners, forced them to look for pretexts to get away. Some evenings, when we sat quietly by ourselves, Peggy would say to me, "Timmy'll never have friends."

I know his teachers felt sorry for Timmy. But they never seemed to know what exactly to do with him. What do you do with a child who is always sullen? "Timmy, please do this. Timmy, do that," his teachers would say to him. And then the anger would begin to catch fire in his eyes, and his lips would tighten. If he was pushed any more, he fell on the floor and stared fixedly at the ceiling. So people left Timmy alone.

It was the same on the playground. Timmy simply wouldn't play if he was told to, if it was somehow expected of him. Instead, he stood in corners, away from the others, his suspicious eyes darting from one side to the other. And the teasing and the taunting came in spells whenever the game grew dull or the children became aware of his presence. Whenever his tormentors came too close, Timmy dropped his chin on his chest, locked his eyes into the ground, and tightened his little hands into fists.

One day, I carved him a little bicycle with a neat little boy riding on it, cap and shorts and all. Peggy hugged me with joy and we made love even before Timmy had a chance to see it. The bicycle and passenger was a hit with Timmy, and we were the greatest of friends from that moment onwards. "Timmy, be a good boy," I said. "I will. I will."

Several weeks later, as we were preparing to drive home from a ball game, and Chris and Dennis were showing off their bikes to the others, Timmy looked out of the car, pulled out of his pocket the wooden bike I had given him, looked at it and said, "1 wonder if I'll ever have a bike like Denny. "I doubt if the words were meant for me. But Peggy and I looked at each other, and I knew we'd get him a bike if that was the last thing I did. I let Peggy break the news to him later that night. Timmy was ecstatic.

From the very next day, Timmy began to announce over and over in his class and outside of class that he was going to get himself a Huffy. With great pride he would then describe — to no one in particular - where he'd go riding. Yes, he'd be faster than a speeding bullet. He'd go roaring through forests so the wild beasts would tremble in fear. He'd go zooming across the highways so others would pull up in amazement and let him pass. His fellow classmates heard him and laughed, so Dennis told me later. But Timmy didn't seem to mind. For he was laughing too. From the day his mother promised him the bike, Timmy wrapped himself up in this indestructible euphoria. His teachers marvelled at the change.

We all began to notice how much Timmy now smiled. The teachers talked about it, wondering how his dark, brooding face could suddenly have become so bright and engaging. Timmy started to talk to others. Dennis would come back from school and tell us about them. The first time Timmy came to our house, Katarina said she had fallen in love with him.

Out on the playground, he walked up to teachers and clusters of children and told them his favorite stories of monsters. Dark, hairy monsters that lay in wait in silent forests where the leaves were so thick and green that the sun was almost invisible. They told me Timmy's voice quivered with excitement as he told his tales, punctuating them with deep growls, screams, and wild, trailing howls. There grew up a fraternity around him. The kids listened intently, often adding their own twists and turns to the stories. The teachers encouraged Timmy in this, and discussed his transformation over coffee and sandwiches during breaks. The strange thing was that Peggy hadn't gotten round to buying the bike. Like me, she too was short on savings.

Timmy didn't stop on the playground. His stories began to find their way into the classroom. When one of the monsters leaped from the topmost branch of a twisted oak tree right in the path of his unstoppable Huffy, the turmoil and chaos that followed proved too much for the class. The teacher had no idea whether to ask Timmy to stop or let him go on. The teacher's aides stood helplessly by. The other children decided to do their own things and the class was a wreck.

The first few times Timmy was asked to stop, he fell down on the floor as usual. But he wouldn't lie still any more. Instead, he kicked his heels alternately on the floor and caused such a racket that his stories seemed better in comparison. So Timmy was allowed to go on with his stories in class. This pleased him no end, although confusion reigned in the minds of his teachers and their helpers.

Peggy and I continued to see each other. Fall came and went, and the fear and anger surrounding Eva and her sleeping pills. Even in the heart of winter, Timmy's excitement remained undimmed. The bike was nowhere in sight, but he was on a high. Peggy had told him there wouldn't be a bike before spring, before the sales started. That made no difference to Timmy. The sidewalks were icy, the streets lined with mud-spattered banks of snow. Timmy rode through it all. One day he walked into class with a crazy limp. "What happened?" everybody cried. Timmy replied that a monster car had collided with his Huffy. He went into graphic details of how the blood poured out of his wounds, how quickly the snow turned red, how he leaped onto his magnificent Huffy and chased the car to the far end of Main Street and shot the driver through the heart. And how his mother found out but said nothing.

"You had better let the wounds heal before you set out on another bicycle adventure," said one teacher, half hoping there'd be a lull in Timmy's stories in the weeks ahead. Such advice made no difference to Timmy. The limp disappeared, but Timmy kept reeling off his stories day after day as if his very life depended on it.

Thanks to Dennis, the story of Timmy and his limp found its way into Peggy's ears. She was angry, and Timmy was fearful of the consequences. He believed that his mother knew everything. Even his most improbable stories, his mother knew all about them. Timmy didn't get strapped or slapped. He never did. Instead, Peggy made him kneel in front of a small crucifix on the wall and ask God's forgiveness for being bad, for lying about the limp. Peggy had made Timmy do this in the past for being bad. This was the ultimate punishment, and Timmy apparently hated it with a passion. His anger would linger for days. This time we heard about it. The anger exploded in school as he unwrapped his sandwiches at lunch. He'd look hard at the sandwiches and scream how he hated them, how he'd love to shove them down his mother's throat when he got home. For the first few days the lunch-room attendant grew alarmed every time Timmy threw a tantrum over his food. But there was nothing wrong with the sandwiches, and after a while nobody took any notice.

But Peggy heard about it, and she did. There were many more kneelings before the crucifix. It only made matters worse. I got into a terrible argument with Peggy and didn't see her for days. But I needed some-one to talk to. There was a wall of silence between me and Eva and the children seemed to have lost their voice. Peggy I wanted to talk to. Timmy I could always talk to.

Peggy called me one day a couple of weeks later to say Timmy was really depressed. He was staying out of trouble but sitting in front of the TV all evening and all day weekends. I couldn't stand it any more. Finally, I showed up on their doorstep the next weekend with a shining Huffy.

There was no jubilation when Timmy finally came face to face with his Huffy. Of course, there was plea-sure written all over his face, but the excitement was tightly controlled to the point where I almost thought he was subdued. He was not. Later that night, when Peggy thought he was fast asleep, Timmy crept out of his bed and went down into the basement. Peggy hap-pened to find a light burning in the stairs and went down to investigate. There was Timmy in his pajamas, sprawled beside his Huffy, his nose touching the front wheel, transfixed by the gleaming machine. Timmy never heard his mother behind him. Peggy went back upstairs as quietly as she had come down.

Timmy learned to ride his bike quickly. The house had a large back yard. Every evening, Katarina and I would help him practice there. Timmy seemed to live for these moments. He didn't say much to me on these evenings. Most of his words seemed to be for Katarina, his face flushed with excitement as he strained his muscles to master the machine. Miraculously, there was laughter and whoops of joy one day when he broke free from my arms and pedalled away on his own. There were hugs and kisses all around. Still, it would be weeks before Peggy would allow him to ride out of the house by himself.

Timmy tended to be forgetful rather than disobedient. So Peggy allowed Katarina to ride with him in the side street and to make it a point to warn him repeatedly where the side street ended and Main Street began. He was not to go out of the side street. Yes, yes, Timmy nodded his head. He understood. But he fretted to be on his own.

Spring came and the trees were heavy with leaves. The woods were full of wild flowers and birds. Flocks of geese squawked in the lake and along the paths. Timmy kept asking when he would be allowed to ride his Huffy into the woods.

"Never on your own," warned Peggy, for that meant riding along Main Street.

The days grew long. Almost every evening, Katarina or I or Peggy was able to ride with Timmy to the edge of the woods. All spring, Timmy was a different kid in school. He was totally happy. He seemed to be living in a different world. He still had his stories to tell, but there was a difference. Now there were stories of rabbits, of ducks, sparrows and cardinals, of brambles and four-leafed clovers. Somehow, the Huffy receded into the background, no longer interesting in itself but as an extension of his own self.

Summer was always a busy season at the store. Katarina was busy with her basketball. Peggy too found it difficult to get back home for a quick ride with Timmy before dark. There still remained the weekends for that, but Timmy found it impossible to hide his restlessness during the week. Every morning, before setting off for school, he would ask Peggy if she wouldn't come home early as she used to in the past.

"Be a good boy, Timmy," said Peggy. "I'll try my best." Timmy decided he couldn't wait for Peggy, or for me or Katarina. One day he headed for the woods on his own, through the sleepy side street on which he lived, and up Main Street. Timmy never made it past the Town Hall. A cruising car killed him on the spot. They found him clutching my carved bicycle in his pocket.

The cathedral was full of Timmy's friends, friends he never seemed to have known. A mountain of flowers and wreaths surrounded his little coffin as they carried him to the nearby cemetery. It was a clear summer day and the sun was a ball of fire. The shadows fell darkly across the spotless lawns and paths. Even the wind stood still so that not a single flower, a single leaf, moved out of place. They laid the body down in the ground and one by one family and friends scattered dust and flowers over the coffin. Peggy went back into the car to look out with vacant eyes at the lovely day. Katarina and I lingered by the coffin until I pulled the carved bicycle out of my pocket and placed it on the coffin, We stood there under an enormous tree for a long time. Katarina cried her heart out. I looked at Eva standing in the distance, and then I looked at Peggy sitting in the car. I knew I had lost them both.

18

Why is it that I can't find Harry when I need him the most? It has been days, weeks, since the trial ended. What's going on. Why do I feel so lost? Well, at least I owe it to Harry to try and explain what happened on the night of November 2. As you can see, I am back home and should be managing to function more or less. But I am not.

We sat down on the steps of his mother's home, a six-pack of beer separating us. As it grew dark and silent, Hans told me things he had been unable to tell the other evening. I listened. His voice rose and fell. Sometimes he came close to screaming in the night. But there was no one around, except his mother in the family room.

Don't worry about her, he said. She lives in a world of her own. She's lived there ever since my father disappeared or got killed. The war toughened her. I was something of a sentimental person when I decided to leave Munich in search of her. I felt sorry for her when I found her in Wiesbaden. Soon it was she who was feeling sorry for me.

I let him go on. I don't think I came close to interrupting him ever.

You see, he began, on November 1 I was in Russia. I was at Kursk to begin with. Then I went to Vorkuta, and finally to Yercevo. I was led into a room which had no ventilation whatsoever. I had a terrible night.

The camp staff were not on the job the following day, so I hardly had anything to eat all morning. I decided to walk around the camp perimeter but found the people rather hostile. So I returned to the bunk and decided to read some of the material they had handed over to us as we came. But I had a hard time concentrating. It would now seem that my eye glass formula was badly out of date.

I heard voices on a loudspeaker booming across the camp. It sounded like people were being harangued by voices that roared, and gigantic crowds were chanting back. Through a hole above my bunk, I saw a small crowd of people marching outside with red banners and flags. I had no idea what they were saying, but whatever it was they seemed to be enjoying it.

By sometime in the late morning or early afternoon I was going crazy from the loudspeakers and the lack of ventilation in my room. So I walked out of the barracks, turned right, and ran straight into the crowd waving flags and banners. They began giving me a lot of dirty, aggressive looks or at least it seemed that way. I couldn't take it for too long. So I turned around and headed back to my room.

A bunch of what I would guess were teenagers or young adults — may be twelve to twenty of them (I'm not at all sure as to numbers) — started pointing at me, then yelling names, although I don't know exactly what. Naturally, I started walking a lot faster. I have the impression a few of these people started throwing rocks or dirt. Suddenly, I got a shove from behind and felt like they were closing in around.

I panicked and ran. Got followed with a lot of yelling and taunting. I was scared to hell. Some of the men were a little ahead of me, and some were beside and behind. There were some grabbing at me, but I can't remember too much. This last part is pretty muddled in my mind.

They obviously weren't committed to do me serious harm. It would have been easy enough for them to have done so. Perhaps they just wanted to have some fun making the German scum look like a fool. But I wasn't thinking along those lines then. I just kept running. I felt physically beaten. Once upon a time I had been a good to indifferent athlete, but Russia has taken its toll. The running was way beyond my capacity.

I stumbled through the barracks and flung myself on my bunk. I must have fallen deeply asleep for fifteen or twenty minutes. But I awoke very violently, and it was at that time that the cycle of my conditions or symptoms commenced, eventually leading me from one prison to the other. Without tiring you with extraneous personal information, I might roughly summarize these symptoms as follows: A high tension, 'buzzey' and 'fuzzey' sensation, as if my head was charged with static electricity. Nausea and dizziness. Uncomfortable hot and cold flashes and shaking. An intense drowsiness with much uncontrollable yawning, big gaps in chains of thought, sentences, and so on. Extremely deep sleep, but for only five or ten minutes, followed by an extremely violent and sudden awakening. Loss of sense of smell and taste. Pressure and throbbing in temple area and great restlessness. A very volatile theatre in my mind, full of crazy themes, ranging from the possible to the absurd, of which I will spare you the details. A virtual forest fire of raging and contending paranoid ideas, and a suffocating physical emotion of horror and dread.(Am I using the word 'paranoid' right? The bastards have drilled it through my head). I could actually taste this feeling of doom, which was the worst part of the whole experience. I found it extremely difficult to be objective about anything. At times I could see, hear, and remember with extraordinary clarity. Then a few minutes later I could not concentrate well enough to understand what was being said to me, or make sense of my own conversation.

I was having the same problems when I ended up in Kingston on November 2. I had just had a raise. I had drunk too much with the boys. The room began to spin around my head. I saw a lot of uniformed Russians coming in and out of the room. On one of my wretched swings through the room, I complimented one of them on his elegant and handsome uniform. He had good English but zero sense of humour. So I had a bunch of them staring me down and asking, "Are you German? Are you American?" With my head buzzing wildly already, I felt about as stupid and defenceless as a person can feel.

But the real trouble was not the chase, and certainly not the Russians — although they do scare the hell out of me. The trouble was what my mind was beginning to do to me, shut up alone in a very hot, stuffy, unventilated room, with X number of hours to kill before morning and no conceivable way of getting to sleep. That was the first of a series of absolutely hellish nights.

My confusion was great, but dared not stop him now. In spite of everything, Hans had a grasp of detail that I found awesome. There were times when his voice rose too high, when his dark eyes became somewhat unfocused, that I came close to interrupting him. But I checked myself just in time. He held me spellbound.

I hoped that my emotional problem would go away once it was morning, he said. But you, my dear Harry, ruined it all. Morning never came. I heard your voice ringing in the night: TO DISREGARD THE LAWS OF OUR BLOOD IS TO DENY GOD'S ORDER IN THIS WORLD AND TO VIOLATE HIS COMMAND. Blood, Harry? And then you cried out: OUR NATION'S ONLY TRUE POSSESSION IS IT'S GOOD BLOOD. Which nation, Harry? What am I doing to myself? Again you cried: ALL PROGRESS CAN BEGIN ONLY BY ELIMINATING THE INFERIOR, AND BY INSISTING ON PROVEN BLOOD. Look where I have fallen! I am the SUB-MAN, in your own words, am I not?

Yes, morning never came. Tulla led me by the hand from room to room. Raising my hands, forcing them down, over and over and over again. I was so fearful once, so afraid. But then it was as if nothing had happened. Everything continued more or less as before. It was as if I was the instrument, not the axe they were waving back and forth in the courthouse. Then I was nothing, like the knife you put down, still, unmoving, incapable of acting on its own.

My first glimpse of Tulla here stirred me, disturbed me, and reminded me of my shame. Soon these stirrings turned to raging storms in my head. That's when I started to really drift apart from Eva. By then I had begun to see relationships as only worth the length of time they survived. Years may be if one was lucky, a week, even a single night. So it did not come as a great shock to me when they rushed Eva to the emergency to pump out all the pills she had swallowed in trying to kill herself. I remembered telling myself it was a strange way to close a chapter just when another was about to begin. Strange and lucky. But it didn't happen that way. I kept dreaming it would. I kept hoping it would.

Throughout the trials, they shielded her and kept her in the shadows. It's true our affair had cooled off for good. But she gave me some letters to mail around this time. As I look back over them, I'm beginning to believe there probably was something of a conspiracy surrounding her. This is a nut-house for sure. One big, happy nut-house. I'd be the first to admit there were times when I mistook Peggy for Tulla. You see, like Tulla she brought music into my life, brought me close to a child's world. It made me alive once again, made me feel complete. Like Tulla she lost her child. Like Tulla she lost her mind.

I don't quite remember where I kept them, but you should see her letters. I never told Piscitelli about them. I know my life is not worth preserving. I wouldn't lift a finger to save myself. You have tried to save me, to protect me - it's all a game for people who write in the papers, for people who argue in courtrooms. I could never shame Peggy to save my hide.

I know I cannot live my dream forever. I was a toymaker once. Now I smash them to extinction. And that must certainly be why I am being persecuted in my new country. For being a toymaker. Why are they doing this to me?

Harry might have been able to make sense out of all this. Harry has been a good friend to me. There was something fanatical, religious about him. He would surely have told me to dispense justice in my own mind, if you know what I mean. What I am going to tell you is that I've decided to pass my own sentence. Piscitelli's fancy logic cannot touch my dreams, my nightmares. The Judge's kindness lies locked out of my sleep. And that's where the trouble lies.

But the children were no dream. I would've named Katarina Tulla but Eva wouldn't hear of it. My Katarina was a beautiful girl, her blue eyes set over cheeks forever in a blush. She was a prisoner of her mortal self and I wanted to set her free. I wanted to preserve her innocence for all times, like the Elizabeth from my very first encounter with the opera. There was such tenderness in her face, as if she was asking why I was punishing her so. I think I held her in my arms and explained that one must do what one has to. For I was with her in a circle of fire, my own private hell, and the bed had suddenly turned into a bed of solid rock.

It was my way of returning to my God. Through a storm of pain, the opiate of the gods. That's how they revive themselves, you know. Without pain, who would ever believe in them? It's farcical, but believable. Wotan's garden, his kingdom, should probably be set in flames. But who will throw the first burning log into Valhalla?

19

I never saw Hans alive again. After the funeral, his mother gave me a letter he had written to me. I did not open the letter till now, until I had put the story together as I think Hans would've liked me to. His piles of garbage next to Piscitelli's. Alternate piles neatly arranged. A story for his beloved Valkyrs, to be read from the skies, from where the piles would all seem as one.

I am squirming back in time, pushing through rotten, crumbling pieces of dirt like a worm. I have so much trouble forming my thoughts these days, he wrote. Not too good in English, a bad speller. With the muscles in my fingers tightening, hesitating, I can see it's going to take me a long time to get through this. Yes, you've been kind to me, Harry.

As I look up, the garage looks more decrepit inside than I can remember. Pop bottles, stacks of newspapers, pieces of broken machinery, and empty oil cans. Half the floor is littered with this junk. In the other half, there's a ghostly, dust-covered Plymouth, full of cobwebs inside, its rusted wheel rims eating away at the flat, cracked tires. Through it all, a musty, cold smell rises from the floor, hovers around the walls and creeps under the coil of rope hanging from the central beam under the roof. I wish I could tell you more, Harry.

I liked the article you wrote about me in The Enterprise a few days ago, Hans wrote. In fact, he said he loved the piece. I've read it so often, I guess it ought to stick in my mind permanently. Then his words started to wander.

He seemed to be addressing someone beyond me. So flattering, so complimentary, said his letter. You wrote it, didn't you, Harry? I'm touched. My eyes are clouding over with tears. Suddenly, I seem to remember every word I've ever spoken, every word spoken to me, spoken of me. I feel a sudden impulse to rush out of the garage, to run into the house and take my mother in my arms. I know she's sitting in her rocking chair by the living room window, a bit like Grandma, staring outside, but seeing nothing. I wonder how many years she must have spent like that. You know, Harry, as I look up at the naked light bulb over my head, I see the yellow rope coiled like a snake around the beam. I see its eyes and am hypnotized by them. I think they're your eyes.

I guess it was the written word Hans was never any good at. Was it him or I? I was starting to forget whether the voices he had told me about were in his head or mine. Now there were voices swarming inside my head. This was no simple matter for a journalist taught to be objective. I'll never forget them. The half-formed screams, the sudden gasp of death. I'll remember these to my grave. All the dead I've ever seen, have ever known, they seem to be rising before my eyes. They're telling me things they had wanted to say in life, but never found the time. Others repeat words they had actually said, accusingly once, with malice in their hearts. I can look into their hearts and can tell if they're friends or enemies. All enemies, every one of them. You were my only friend, Harry, Hans said to me. But were you real?

Peggy never forgave me for Timmy's death. One day she told me I was no better than an Eichmann, a Mengele. It seemed Eva and Katarina too had passed their sentence on me. Oh yes! I found Peggy's letters among some of my junk that Mother had stashed away. Peggy would have me look them over and mail them as a final gesture of our lost friendship. I did nothing. Perhaps I should've sent them. Do what you wish with them. Just don't hurt her. They're coming to you as Exhibit 1 and Exhibit 2. Sound familiar?

EXHIBIT 1

27 September 1966

34 Adams Street,
Brockton, Mass. 02373

General Accounting Office
441 G Street, N.W.
Washington, D.C. 20458

As egg mother of thousands, I am asking GAO for a general accounting of my children whose lives were ended, shortened or maimed in the hands of United States employees or citizens.

Human beings are resources, too. If there are white papers or other arguments creating, justifying or defending agency, military, or United States policy in inducing disease, torturing (tormenting), maiming or killing my offspring, please send me copies. I want to evaluate who sold whom what bill of goods, or whether constitutional protections have so degenerated that no such rhetoric was even necessary.

In terms of survival, what number and percentage of those conceived are still alive? What number and percentage were sold abroad so no statistics are directly available? If not directly available, what are the reasonable estimates? Of those who died, what percentage died before

(Continued)

birth? Whether death occurred before or after birth, I want to know the manner and agency of death.

Please specify the sex of the killers of my children as well as military and agency affiliations. For example: F/Navy/NSA or M/ GAO/Airforce, or whatever. If the manner of death was prolonged, as death by torture (torment), please specify the kind of torture, whether it was used on that subject before, the percentage of people of that age surviving that kind of torture, and the risks of associated damage other than death.

Please specify unusual statistics. For example, some of my children were maimed as embryos. Many lab workers reported that General Wilson used to eat some of my children. A concerned nun and lab worker whose (1963?) death certificate read 'natural causes', when laid out in the South Easton Sacred Heart Chapel, was found to have a bullet hole in the back of her neck. It was to curb just such barbarism that American civilization hammered out the constitution on the anvil of the old legal order.

Thanking you for making the fate of my children part of the public record, I am,

Sincerely,
Peggy Constanza

EXHIBIT 2

27 October 1966

34 Adams Street,
Brockton, Mass. 02373

Dear Senator,

In 1965 — counting the Chinese and their high tech facility at twin-making — knowledgeable insiders claimed I had over 14,000 children. This fertile output came in response to my IQ early estimated in the 225-240 range and the evidence of siddhis some thought inheritable.

My use by force as breeding stock did not go without protests. In 1948, at the age of five, I proposed that my eggs be distributed through the United Nations. This provoked laughter among those who were seizing my eggs and creating an international black market for their distribution.

Responding to threats of sterilization, institutionalization, further torture, and chemically induced mental and emotional depression, I made a deal with my *bete noir*. Around 1950, in the presence of Department of Defense observers, the now NSA General Donald Wilson and I made a contract. I would give my eggs free provided he never — directly or indirectly — maimed, tortured, murdered, or used my children for

(Continued)

biological and biochemical experiments, whether before or after birth. If not, I would be awarded half of his resources, under all social security numbers he uses, before taxes.

As the world suspects, seldom has a contract been more violated. Thanks to kindness in the upper echelons of government, now that my chemical bondage has not been removed, I want to determine the fate of my children and compare their treatment at various times by various nations.

If the legal order in the United States is equitable, I should obtain settlements from those Generals and other heads responsible for significant harm to me and my children. Given an accounting of my children, I hope to be in a position to respond to humanity's children at large as well as my own.

But I will be prone to do this according to those countries that have been most civil to my children. For example, in 1965 the U.S. survival rates to adulthood were estimated at 49%, the Chinese at 93%, and I suspect the Arabs and Germans are in between.

Enclosed is a copy of a letter querying the United States. The Boston branch of General Accounting Office told me that pressure would have to come from Senators and Congressmen before they can do anything, that they keep records only two years, and that they passed on some old records to the Department of Justice.

(Continued)

But long-term breeding records are stored somewhere. The Supreme Court has now declared that matters of fact cannot be classified insofar as they are part of the public record.

Any help you could give to this information gathering would be appreciated, as my time is limited. Against my will, radioactive materials have been placed in my body.

Thanking you, I remain,

Sincerely,
Pegg'y Constanza

As I read them over, there is one part of me that wants to laugh at them. There's another part that starts running scared, because it may not be totally fanciful after all. I have heard enough of what we Germans are supposed to have done to others. I'm not so sure others are wholly incapable of such terrible acts.

What is this thing called pain? I stay awake at night, I stare at the darkness and ask, what is it? I think of Katarina's, Tulla's, Eva's, Peggy's, and I wonder where it all ends up. What is merciful about pain? How come some of us never see the merciful face of God? We are what we are. We must live and die with what we are born with. I can only serve the deserving. But there are some born not to be served. Some whose souls are timid, blood impure. I cannot change what I am. I cannot change myself and spurn the strength I was born with, the mind and body of a man.

Oh Tulla! I would've followed you to the ends of the earth. Too late. I realized too late you weren't of the earth. At your awakening, the wind worked itself into such a fury that the dark clouds disappeared in fear and the sun appeared. I thought I could hold on to your beauty, your memory, forever. And now I can't see you any more, Harry. I don't even remember what you looked like. I don't need your pity. Save your tears. I walked around in heaven once. But you've delivered me into hell. Bin ich nun frei? wirk-lich frei? Ruinen-mauschen, they deserve to die. Every one of them.

Allers was ist, endet. Ruhe, Ruhe, du Gott.